Books by Charles Sheehan-Miles

Thompson Sisters
A Song for Julia
Falling Stars
A View From Forever
Just Remember to Breathe
The Last Hour

Thompson Sisters / Rachel's Peril
Girl of Lies
Girl of Rage
Girl of Vengeance

America's Future
Republic
Insurgent

Nocturne (with Andrea Randall)

Prayer at Rumayla
A Novel of the Gulf War

Saving the World on Thirty Dollars a Day:
An Activist's Guide to Starting, Organiz-
ing and Running a Non-Profit Organization

Become A Full-Time Author (with Andrea Randall)

A VIEW FROM FOREVER

A Thompson Sisters Novel

Charles Sheehan-Miles

www.sheehanmiles.com

Published by Cincinnatus Press
PO Box 814
South Hadley, Massachusetts
United States of America

ISBN: 9781632021182

v04152015

CHAPTER ONE

No politics on the first date (Dylan)

THE WOMAN BEHIND the counter has hair cut about to her chin, longer at the front and shorter in the back. It's dyed a bronze color, and I can't tell her age or even her general appearance because the makeup she wears is thick as wood-grain veneer on cheap particleboard. Her eyelids, thick with glittery blue eyeshadow, flutter as she talks to a man behind the counter who isn't wearing an airline uniform. Actually, he doesn't appear to be there for any other purpose than to flirt with the woman.

"Excuse me," I say.

She ignores me and continues to smack her gum.

I like to give everyone the benefit of the doubt. But if this is how everyone is going to behave in New York, I'd just as soon go back to the South.

"Excuse me, Miss?" I try my best to contain my irritation. I can't go as far as Ma'am, though my Mom wouldn't approve. Mamma always told me to keep up my best manners even if the world was coming to an end.

"What?" The look she gives me is anything but accommodating. Is it the Southern accent? Or because I'm a teenager? Or is she just normally rude? Who knows?

Impossible to tell. What I do know is that she's making me angry.

"I was on Flight 658, along with my friends." I gesture to the others from the Atlanta delegation. "None of our luggage has shown up at the baggage claim."

She gives me a briefly scornful look, then picks up a phone and dials. "Yeah, Gary? This is Bethany, in Terminal 4. Yeah, that's me. I got some teenagers here, they say their luggage didn't come off Flight 658."

She pauses and tilts her head. "Uh huh… uh huh …. Yeah? Well, that's a bummer. All right."

None of that sounds good. She hangs up the phone. It's clear she'd rather be flirting with the guy, or doing a crossword puzzle, or just about anything else other than talking with me. "Sorry, but security diverted one load of luggage at Hartsfield." She doesn't pronounce the -R in Hartsfield, instead saying it like *Hahhtsfield*. She continues. "It should catch up with you in the next day or so. You gotta fill out some paperwork, and give it to the TSA supervisor. I'll call him over." She's already taking out the paperwork. A lot of it.

Forty minutes later—without luggage—we join up with the students from the other groups. Except for Tameka, I haven't had a chance to get to know any of the others in my group. Tameka lives in Virginia Highlands, a neighborhood in northeast Atlanta, and goes to Grady High School. She's a junior and heavily involved in sports and academics. They all are. The five of us had to attend a dinner where we gave short introductions a couple of weeks ago—these four girls are all high achievers at their schools. It makes me feel like I'm not up to scratch—a year ago I was a high school dropout and I still don't understand why they let *me* on this trip.

As we approach the ground transportation area, next to the baggage claim, I see a woman holding a large sign: Council of Great City Schools Foreign Exchange Program. She is medium height with blonde hair, cut in a relatively short style with bangs. I'd guess she's around thirty-five years old. She waves as she sees us approach. I wrinkle my nose—this part of the airport smells vaguely like piss and old-stale cigarette smoke.

A group of twelve or so teenagers stands in a loose semicircle around the woman. Harried and tired passengers stream by on their way to wherever they are going. One girl stands to the left of the group and a few feet away as she talks on what looks like an iPhone. I've never *seen* one before—they just came out a few months ago and no one in my circle can afford toys like that. Her bags are on the floor and she has a pained expression on her face. What catches my eyes is her long, luscious-looking brown hair, slightly olive skin, and how her sweater hugs her upper body.

"No, Mom. We haven't even left the airport yet." Silence, then the girl rolls her eyes, giving me a look at her deep green irises. "Of course. Yes. Yes. I will. Okay."

A crease forms in the center of her forehead as her eyebrows draw together. "No, I don't think I'll have a chance to see Carrie, we've got a pretty full schedule before we leave for Tel Aviv. But I'll call her if I get some free time."

When her eyes swing toward me, I quickly look away. Then I nearly jump when someone speaks almost in my ear. "*Jaysus*, she's hot, isn't she?"

I jerk back. The speaker is a guy with brown curly hair. He looks like a caricature of a teenager. Basketball-player tall, but with arms and legs more like a stick figure than a human, all elbows and knees. I'm not really up on the latest fashion, though a lot of my classmates back home are—homelessness, even for a brief period, gives you an appreciation of having any clothes at all. But this kid clearly hasn't ever missed a meal, and he's decked out in an array of corporate logos and brand names.

I instantly dislike him—then I back that off. I'm here to learn, not to judge the other kids. I know better than to judge people just by their appearance.

"Yeah," I murmur. The girl is *way* the hell out of my league.

"I'm Mike," he says. "From Chicago."

"Dylan. I'm from Atlanta."

"Oh, yeah? Southern boy, huh?"

"Through and through," I reply. Is he serious?

He looks at me and asks, "What's your politics?"

"What?"

"You know. Democrat? Republican?"

I snort. "I don't talk politics on the first date."

He chuckles.

"Okay," says the woman, raising her voice in an effort to be heard over the other travellers, announcements and random noises in the terminal. "I'm Marie Simpson; I'll be one of your chaperones for the next several weeks.

Please let me get everybody's names. We've got the Chicago and San Francisco and Atlanta groups here?"

She begins to read out names, starting with the students from Atlanta. Tameka is first, then two of the other girls, then me. A few minutes later, after she gets the names of the five students from Chicago, she moves on to the San Francisco group—five of them.

The San Francisco group has four girls—including the one I've been trying to not obviously stare at. The fifth kid in the group is a vaguely Asian or Pacific Island looking guy. Then *she* responds to her name, which I hear for the very first time.

Alexandra Thompson.

What could go wrong? (Alex)

You would think that telling my mother we had a busy schedule in New York, and that I didn't think I'd have the opportunity to get in town to see Carrie, would have been enough to end the discussion. Maybe you would think that my mother would actually *listen* to me. Or consider that I have things I'm supposed to be doing on this trip other than running off to see Carrie. You would *think* that it would be good enough that I'm going to visit Carrie for three days when this trip is over.

If you thought any of that, you would be wrong.

My mother always, *always*, calls at the wrong time. Or says the wrong thing. Or just gets too involved in a way I don't understand. Today is no different. I'm standing, listening as she talks (it's not a conversation—she speaks, I listen). On and on. How to behave while in New York, and further, how to be behave when I arrive in Tel Aviv. Dress conservatively. Everything I do will reflect on my father. Things to watch out for. *Blah blah blah.*

The whole time she talks, I keep seeing this boy out of the corner of my eye. He is medium height and has hair a bit on the long side, messy muddy brown, not the sculpted, highly-cut-and-cared-for haircuts of most of the boys I know. He doesn't appear to care the least about fashion—unlike the stupidly manicured boy who stands next to him with his *oh-so-carefully* unbuttoned Hollister shirt. Instead, *this* boy wears a grey t-shirt, blue jeans and a pair of what looked like well-worn work boots. He has a canvas backpack and carries a guitar case in his right hand.

I try not to let him see I'm looking at him, at the same time my mother's voice gets higher and higher pitched.

"*Mom!*" I finally say. "I gotta go. I'll call you tomorrow, okay?"

"Young lady, you call me when you get settled in your room tonight. I need to know you are safe."

"Of *course* I'm safe. What could go wrong?"

She doesn't answer that, of course. Let's face it—my mother could conjure a thousand reasons I should stay home, a thousand things that could go wrong. It's a wonder she let me go on this trip at all. Ever since Julia and Crank got married, and Carrie announced she was going to major in *biology* of all things, Mom and Dad have become that much more controlling. I don't even need to bother looking at a selection of schools. I'm going to Harvard (like Julia, like my Dad), then the Fletcher School (like Dad) and then into the Foreign Service, whether I like it or not.

Except, that isn't what I want to do at all.

Sometimes I envy my older sisters, both of whom found the strength to defy our parents. Julia even went beyond the personal and into the political—she publicly backed Barack Obama's campaign for President, an action which made minor news since our father is an advisor to John McCain. When Julia came through town a few weeks ago and visited for dinner, she and my father maintained a stiff and hostile silence for the entire meal, an experience which nearly gave my mother a nervous breakdown. It was irritating—I love my sisters, but sometimes Julia sucks all of the oxygen out of the room.

I miss Julia and Carrie and Andrea. It's just me and the twins at home most of the time, and sometimes it's oppressive.

Not much later, I'm sitting alone, staring out the window as the bus leaves the airport and heads on toward Hunter College, where we'll be staying the next three days. The fall weather outside doesn't have the glorious, colorful look you might see in the mountains of Northern California—instead, it just looks dreary and grey. The sky threatens more rain and that suits my mood perfectly.

All the time, I'm fully aware of the boy in the grey t-shirt and jeans who took a seat at the front of the bus across the aisle across from me. I heard his name earlier, when they were taking the roll. *Dylan Paris.* It's an intriguing name, but names tell me nothing really. And he looks different than the others... somehow older. I want to find out *who he is*, but there's no way to ask without being very, very awkward.

Instead, I stare out the window, and think about how weird my mother has been the last few days, and how relieved I am to be getting away from home for a while. A truck roars by, its diesel thrum vibrating the heavy traffic around it. I can smell exhaust fumes and the tendrils of cigarette smoke from desperate smokers huddled under the awnings, trying to stay out of the rain.

Everyone else on the bus has grouped up and spends the ride into New York talking. But Dylan Paris just sits there quietly looking out the window. Who is he?

Chapter Two

Mom's gone off her meds (Alex)

A LEXANDRA?" MARIE SIMPSON, one of the counselor/chaperones, knocks on the door and pokes her head in the room.

"I go by Alex, actually." I respond.

Technically this isn't true. I've gone by *Alexandra* my entire life. But something compelled me to introduce myself to my two roommates last night as Alex. This is the first time I've ever travelled without my family; the first time I've ever been anywhere on my own. Somehow, introducing myself as *Alex* makes me feel almost like a different person. So, Alex it is.

"Sorry," Mrs. Simpson responds. "Alex. Anyway, small change of plans. You won't be required to attend tonight's reception."

"Oh?" I actually *wanted* to attend the reception—all day long we'd sat through lecture after lecture, and occasionally I'd sensed the eyes of that boy on me. But there hadn't been an opportunity to be introduced. "If it's all the same to you, I'd like to...." I trail off, realizing this is absurd. The reception must have been cancelled, because there's no reason I'd be singled out to—

"Actually, we received a call from—I believe it was your father—Ambassador Richard Thompson?"

I close my eyes, feeling a sudden mix of resignation and anger flash through me. "Yes. He's my father."

"He was apparently outraged that you weren't being allowed to see your sister while you were in the city."

I frown. "I'd love to see my sister, but I assumed there wasn't going to be time."

A slightly disapproving frown passes over her face. "Well, now there is time."

I sigh. "I didn't ask for this, Mrs. Simpson. I didn't ask for special treatment."

She arches her eyebrows. "Well, then. Your father is a U.S. Ambassador—it wouldn't do to disappoint him now, would it?"

I smile bitterly, thanking God that my roommates weren't in the room to hear all of that. "Of course not. One doesn't disappoint Richard Thompson." Mrs. Simpson's face takes on a sour expression at my sarcastic words.

"I understand your sister is at Columbia University? Your father indicated you would be all right taking a cab?"

"I guess," I reply.

What about when *I'm* disappointed?

I sigh. Whatever. Mrs. Simpson leaves the room, and I glumly change clothes. Twenty minutes later, after texting Carrie for directions, I'm in a New York City taxicab.

I arrive at Jewel Bako in the East Village a few minutes early. I've never been here before, though I've visited Carrie in college a couple of times in the last two years. She directed me here, saying that it was the best sushi in

New York. It's dark already, with winter well on its way, and a light drizzle falls on the city, leaving the streets slick and slightly reflective. A few storefronts line the ground floor of East 5th Street, but this block is mostly residential, though the corner with 2nd Avenue is busy with traffic and noise. The noise drops, however, as I enter the restaurant. Two rows of tables line the walls of the well-lit room, which looks almost like a tunnel because of the curved bamboo ceiling arching over the diners. I unzip my raincoat a few inches as the hostess approaches.

"Two, please, for dinner. My sister made reservations."

When I give her Carrie's name, I'm whisked to a table in the back corner, directly across from the sushi chef. She must be a regular here. I barely have time to sit down when I see her approaching.

Carrie and I couldn't look more different. At a couple of inches over six feet, she's gorgeous—model-thin, always glamorous, even when casual. Tonight she's dressed in jeans, boots and a black raincoat, but somehow she makes it seem like she's walking on a runway. I always feel like I disappear next to her.

I stand and we embrace. She kisses me on the cheek, then as we sit down, she pulls a gift bag out of her purse.

"Happy birthday," she says.

I'm startled. I wasn't expecting anything like that. I smile and take the bag. Inside I find a grey scarf, silk, with fine metallic thread. As I would expect, Carrie's taste is right on—this will match a lot of my clothes.

My birthday isn't actually for another week, but I'm absurdly pleased that she planned ahead.

"That's so sweet," I say.

"You like it?"

"Yes! Thank you so much."

"Oh, Alexandra, it's so good to see you," she says. "I feel like it's been forever."

I nod. "Yeah." Carrie just started graduate school at Columbia, and she spent the summer teaching undergraduate biology courses instead of coming back home to California. "How have you been?"

She shrugs, a mysterious smile on her face. "I've been well. I'm kind of excited: I'm going to be doing a lot more fieldwork this year."

"I missed you this summer," I say. She spent her summer tracking down mountain lions. I spent the summer at home with a mother who has been crazy for the last few months—undoubtedly Carrie knows that. They talk on the phone very frequently. Nor do I tell her that I haven't seen Dad in almost three months—he's been away on a super secret State Department mission of some kind or another. I don't even know what country he's in. But she knows. After all, she's the one who passed down the mantle of *protector* to me, whether I wanted it or not.

"I missed you, too," Carrie says. "It was really weird not coming home this year. Though I have to admit, I love my apartment, and I love the fieldwork. Finally moving out of the dorms was fantastic. Do you think you'll have time to come see it before you leave town?"

I slowly shake my head. "I don't think so, honestly. I'm missing one of the receptions right now, actually."

Carrie gets an odd expression. "Don't look so bummed about it. You've been to enough receptions over the years—I'm glad we got to see each other."

I smile. "I am too. To tell you the truth, it wasn't the reception itself that interested me."

She arches an eyebrow. "Oh? Tell me. Wait... is it... a guy?"

I frown. "Carrie...."

She smiles. "You can tell me anything. Cross my heart." She does, first making a sign of the crucifix, which would drive mother *insane* if she saw it, then she pretends to turn a key in her mouth and throw it away. But we're interrupted when the waitress appears. We order specialty rolls, and Carrie orders white wine for both of us. The waitress gives me a *very* skeptical look, but doesn't ask for ID.

"There is a guy who fascinates me on this trip," I say.

"What's his name? Tell me everything."

"I don't know anything about him," I say. "That's why I'm so intrigued. His name's Dylan Paris—he's a senior, from Atlanta—and that's all I know. He doesn't really talk with anyone."

"Stuck up?"

I shake my head. "The opposite, I think. All of the other guys are preppies. He's not, and I think maybe he's intimidated."

Carrie smiles. "You should take him under your wing then, before you leave for Tel Aviv." Vintage Carrie there, to want to rescue someone.

"Well, I'd have to get up the courage to talk with him first."

She throws her head back and laughs. "You've got a point, sister. Just keep me in the loop. You're running off to a foreign country with a strange guy." She gives the barest of mischievous smile as she says, "It's very romantic."

"He'll probably turn out to be gay," I say with a grimace.

"Most of the good guys are. Enough about that. Catch me up on home, will you?"

I shrug. "Not much to say. Um... let's see... Andrea spent two weeks with us in the summer."

"Oh, good! God, I miss her."

"Me too." Our youngest sister, Andrea, has lived in Spain with our grandmother almost full time for the last couple of years. "You won't believe it when you see her. She's taller than I am already, and looks a *lot* like you did when you were little."

Carrie sits back. "That tall already? What is she, eleven?"

"Ten. And I bet she's going to be just as tall as you are."

"Weird. How did *we* get so lucky?" she asks in a sarcastic tone. "Have you seen Julia?"

I shake my head. Twenty-five year old Julia, our oldest sister, is a law unto herself. "They're on tour again."

"Yeah, I know—I went to the Allan Roark concert last winter; they were opening." She shakes her head. "I'd have liked to have seen Andrea."

"None of us knew she was coming," I reply. "Mom said she wanted it to be a surprise."

"That is so weird," Carrie says.

"No kidding. You know what the latest is? Mom's absolutely *obsessed* with the British Royal family."

"What, William and Kate and all their drama?"

I shake my head. "No—Prince George-Phillip and Lady Anne Davies... she's having a baby soon, apparently."

"Never heard of her. But I know who *he* is, he spoke at my graduation. He was Ambassador to the UN at the time."

"He's second cousin to the Queen?"

"Something like that. Basically, what you're saying is that Mom's gone off her meds."

It takes no more than half a second before I can't contain the laugh. Then both of us are giggling, hard. It's not often I get to spend time with Carrie, and the twins are still in middle school and don't really get some things. I wipe a small tear from my eyes.

"It's so good to see you, Carrie."

She smiles, the warm and loving smile I've always known from my big sister. "It's good to see you, Alexandra. What about you? What's happening in your life? Are you still thinking about Columbia?"

I nod. "Yes. Dad is *not happy* about that. He wants me to go to Harvard."

"It wouldn't be a bad choice," she says. "Though obviously I'm in favor of Columbia."

"I'd be locked into his future, Carrie. I don't want to be a diplomat. I want to live in the same city, not move every three years until the airports and embassies become a blur and I can't remember what year I was in what country. You know?"

She nods. "I do. You know, though, just because you go to Harvard doesn't mean you're committing to his life. Look at Julia. She went off the track *completely.*"

"True," I say. "Though I don't see any rock bands in my future. Dad still hasn't forgiven her."

Carrie shrugs. "He'll come around."

I suppress my doubts. "I'm seriously thinking about law school."

"Yeah?" Carrie looks skeptical. "Like corporate law?"

I shake my head. "No. That sounds horrible. I want to do something meaningful. Can I tell you a secret?"

Looking slightly amused, she nods. I mockingly half whisper, "I want to go to work for the ACLU."

Carrie's eyes widen. Then she snickers. Just once. "Dad would rather you married a punk rocker, I think. Bravo." She's probably right. The American Civil Liberties Union is an organization best not mentioned in our home.

We laugh, hard now, and I find myself wishing my stay in New York was going to be longer—long enough to spend a lot more time with my sister. Even though I hadn't asked for it, in the end I'm grateful my parents got involved and that I got to see her.

With the dawn of redeeming grace (Dylan)

Blah, blah blah.

That's what the speakers have been saying for the last forty-five minutes at the reception at the American-Israel Friendship League.

Blah blah blah.

First they've been thanking people none of us have ever heard of for making cooperation between the two countries possible. A retired ambassador speaks, followed by someone from the Anti-Defamation League, then two speakers from the Council of Great City Schools. On and on and on.

"Check that girl out," Mike from Chicago says, his voice none too quiet. His eyes are on one of the girls from the Milwaukee delegation. She's probably a junior, and she's leaning forward with one knee crossed over the other. She stands out in this crowd of preppies: colorful spiked hair, a black leather jacket and bright pink combat boots. She's cute, really—if anything, she kind of reminds me of Spot, a girl I used to know who hung around the Masquerade and a few other lesser alternative clubs. Spot—I don't know what her real name is—was creative as hell, smart, cute, and addicted to painkillers. Her parents had kicked her out, and there were a few times we ended up shacking up together. Not out of lust or attraction—she was strictly a lesbian—but out of a need to stay warm on cold, homeless nights.

Yes, homeless. See, my Mom is a parent of the tough-love variety, and when I dropped out of high school, she gave me an ultimatum. Go back to school and quit drinking, or get out. I couch surfed for a while—after all, I had plenty of friends. But parents of sixteen year olds become curious—too curious—when a sleepover turns into an extended stay.

I found occasional work in the fall—landscaping, day labor. Show up at the 7-11 in the morning and stand in line with the illegal immigrants and other homeless looking for a day's backbreaking labor for 25 bucks. Then I'd go hang out with the guys and smoke pot.

I met Spot the weekend before Thanksgiving. I was standing with a couple of guys behind the dumpster in the back of the Masquerade having a smoke when I heard a short, muffled scream. I got up and walked down the alley, my friends trailing behind me. In the dark I could barely make out what was happening—a big guy, maybe six feet, and built, was shaking a girl who stood maybe five-feet two and probably weighed 95 pounds. Her head was flopping back and forth as he shook her hard, using his massive strength to shake her like a rag doll.

"Stop!" she squeaked. He pulled his fist way back, about to slug her.

He didn't get to throw the punch: Snatching up a loose brick, I lunged forward and hit him in the back of the head. He went down, and the alley fell silent.

"Mother fuck," one of the guys said. "That's Lonnie Wallace. Dylan, get the fuck out of here before he wakes up. I'm out."

"Who is he?" I asked

"Dealer. Dangerous man. Really dangerous. I'm gone."

I shrugged, then looked at the girl. "You okay?" I asked.

She looked at me, a little dazed. "Yeah," she whispered.

I had my doubts. But I didn't have anywhere safe to take her. "You got any place to go? Someone we can call?"

She shook her head.

I sighed. Then I said, "Let's take a walk. Get away from here. I'm Dylan."

"Spot," she said.

Weird. Whatever. Lot of people used street names. I grabbed her hand and said, "Let's go. I don't want to be here when he wakes up."

"He's got a gun," she said.

Shit.

That changed things, didn't it? I crouched down and touched the guy's shoulder. He wasn't moving. I hoped he wasn't dead. I leaned close enough to see and hear that he was breathing. I rolled him over and, sure enough, a pistol was stuffed in his waistband. Automatic, I guess—I didn't know much about guns other than what I'd seen on television and the one or two times when I was a little kid that my dad took me hunting. But we didn't hunt with automatic pistols.

Dad had taught me basic weapons safety. I slid the pistol out of Asshole's waistband. It took a minute trying to figure out how to eject the magazine, then I found the button and ejected the magazine, then pulled the slide back. The chambered bullet went flying.

"Come on," I said. I left the ammo on the ground and threw the pistol in the dumpster. Just to slow him down, if he ever woke up. Then I grabbed her hand and we ran.

A month later on Christmas Eve, I ran into Spot downtown, not long after the trains stopped running for the night. It was raining and cold, and my jacket did little to keep me dry. I was looking for a good sheltered spot to sleep when I ran into her. We walked together and finally huddled under the bridge under I-20. I'd slept there before, and knew the dozen or so semi-permanent residents who kept tents, clotheslines, mattresses and personal items stored there.

When we got there that night, a blazing fire was going, and two families were huddled around the fire.

"It looks warm," she said.

"Come on, then," I replied, and pulled her over to the fire. I could feel the heat against my skin, and the heat of Spot as she leaned against me.

Sometimes I wanted to track down her asshole father and punch him until he couldn't see. I was just as homeless as Spot was, but I was homeless because of something *I did*—not because of who I was. She, on the other hand, was a good kid with bad parents. They had kicked her out because she was a lesbian. Not because of anything she'd done—they kicked her out because of *who she was.*

That's when it hit me. I could choose to go home any time I wanted. All I had to do was stop the drinking and pot. All I had to do was go back to school.

Spot *couldn't* go home. She had no one.

The mother of one of the two families who lived under the bridge began to sing. Her voice was clear and beautiful and the moment she heard the singing begin, Spot began to shiver. Then to sob.

Silent night, Holy night
All is calm, all is bright
Round yon virgin, mother and child
Holy infant, tender and mild
Sleep in heavenly peace,
Sleep in heavenly peace.

Silent night, Holy night
Son of God, love's pure light
Radiant beams from thy holy face
With the dawn of redeeming grace,
Jesus, Lord at thy birth
Jesus, Lord at thy birth.

Silent night, Holy night
Shepherds quake, at the sight
Glories stream from heaven above
Heavenly, hosts sing Hallelujah.
Christ the Savior is born,
Christ the Savior is born.

I'll be honest. I cried just a little too, as I held Spot and she sobbed. I wished right then that I could find a home for her, find someone who loved her. But it wasn't really feasible. I had no resources, no money. I had *nothing*.

A few weeks later, I had signed up to go back to school. I had quit drinking and cleaned up my act. I had moved back home. And then I had gone looking for Spot. There were a dozen weekends over the months after that, when I went and looked for her, searching at clubs and under bridges—searching everywhere.

But I never saw her again.

Now, I'm slow to come back to the present. Now, my missing friend Spot seems far more real than the kids here in New York.

"Hello?" Mike from Chicago says, waving a hand in front of my face. "Are you awake?" I've heard him introduce himself that way to half a dozen people now. *Hi, I'm Mike. From Chicago.* It's become part of his name.

I shake my head slightly. "Sorry. I guess I was stuck in a memory."

He chuckles. "Must have been a good one."

I don't answer. I go through the motions for the remainder of the reception, listening where I need to and saying what I have to, but never really focused on the present. I'm interested in the foreign exchange program, but sometimes it is difficult to maintain my sense of reality. I'm surrounded by people who think hunger was not being able to get your favorite appetizer and who flaunt clothing which is unimaginably expensive, just because they can. They're public school kids just like I am, but they're public school kids with backgrounds I don't really understand: tutors and test-prep programs, expensive extracurricular activities and parents who sponsor scholarships, academic camps and God only knew what else.

I don't belong there.
I don't belong anywhere.

CHAPTER THREE

Love is Fleeting (Alex)

'VE NEVER TRIED to quantify the number of flights I've taken in my life. After all, I've lived in a lot of places. I might be sixteen, but my father is a U.S. Ambassador. I've lived in San Francisco, Beijing, Brussels, Moscow and Washington, DC. The first flight I remember was in 1994. I was about four years old, and I somehow got separated from my mom and my sisters. I remember wandering through the terminal, and no one spoke English, and everyone looked *huge*, and I cried for Carrie. *None of us ever* cried for our Mom. From what I've heard in the years since, that was during a layover and plane switch in Tokyo—one of the largest airports in the world.

Add up all the places we've lived—plus short trips for holidays—and this is probably the hundredth flight I've been on. Whenever possible, I fly as close to the front of the plane as I can—usually not a problem because when traveling with my father, one travels first class.

Not so on this foreign exchange trip. My seat is on Row 51 in the coach section. That far back in the plane, the left and right rows only have two seats, while the center has four. I'm jammed up next to the window. At least it isn't one of the tiny seats I was forced to ride in on the flight from San Francisco to New York three days ago.

I know, in principle, that people have to ride in coach. *Most* people ride in coach. I've been lucky, *very* lucky, that I've never had to. At least this isn't so bad, unless my seat-mate turns out to be obnoxious. We will see—our group apparently has an entire block covering most of the back of the plane, so it is likely to be another one of the students in our group.

I stuff my handbag under the seat in front of me. It contains two paperback novels, my phone and assorted other junk. I pull out my neck pillow, stuffing it in the back of the seat for whenever I get sleepy, which will likely be soon. The flight is scheduled to leave at ten p.m., with a morning arrival time in Barcelona, where we have a short layover. .

My mother would say I'm dithering: my mind is on the email I'm planning to send to Mike, but I haven't quite organized myself to do it yet, so I'm doing and thinking about everything else.

Michael Harrington comes from an old-money San Francisco family, and his father and my father are … friends? Colleagues? It's hard to know the relationship. But the Harringtons are often guests at our home, and I suppose that it was inevitable that eventually Michael and I would date. Far preferable him than Randy Brewer, who my parents have been pushing on me since the eighth grade. Randy is a sanctimonious prick. Mike, on the other hand is … I don't know. Bland? It's not that he doesn't have a personality—it's just that it isn't all that interesting. He gets okay grades, but isn't brilliant. He plays piano because his mother forces him to have lessons, but he doesn't really care for it.

In truth, it seems like Mike doesn't really care for much of *anything*. He just doesn't have any passion in him. He goes through life knowing that he has a massive trust fund and that he doesn't really have to do much of anything in life to survive. He'll always have his country club memberships and access to the rich and powerful—he'll always *be* rich and powerful, and not through any efforts of his own.

His response? Complete disinterest.

All the same, a few weeks ago, while my parents and his parents were attending some charity auction (I think it was for the San Francisco Opera? Or the Science Museum? I'm not sure which), the two of us were seated together. He was unusually quiet that night, but he finally leaned over and said, "Alexandra... would you like to have dinner with me?"

I didn't point out that we were already having dinner, though I wanted to. Instead, I assented. I don't know why. It wasn't pity, but it wasn't interest either. We went out a few times—dinner, movies, the symphony.

My reaction to his advances? Complete disinterest.

I finally decided last night it was time to let him know. But how? Do I call? Not from Israel. And somehow it feels tacky to just text message or send him a message on Facebook. Which leaves me with email. Impersonal, but not as much as a text. Better than the painfully-awkward, ugly conversation we might have in person. The thing is, I don't really even like Mike. And outside of my relationship with my family, I don't think he really likes me either. Letting him know now will be a blessing in a way. He'll have a few weeks to process it before I return home.

I finally settle back into my seat. The seats around me are filling; the aisle crowded with travelers making their way to their seats.

Then I spot that guy. Dylan Paris, from Georgia.

We still haven't spoken. He carefully makes his way down the aisle, guitar case in his left hand, boarding pass in his right. He looks at his boarding pass with a fierce expression I have some difficulty interpreting, then up to the seat numbers above the row. I watch his eyes move from one seat to the next, rows 48, then 49, 50, then 51. Then his gaze drops to the empty seat next to me—then to me. His eyes widen, just a little bit, then he looks back to the seat next to me. From the looks of it, he is headed right to me.

Less than a minute later the people ahead of him clear out of the way and he drops a worn backpack onto the seat next to me, saying "Hey". The backpack isn't faux-worn, with stone-washed pre-faded fabric and an expensive label. It looks like a second-hand Army backpack, right down to the stenciled name that I know isn't his. "I'm Dylan."

Then he smiles, a warm looking slightly sideways grin that barely shows his teeth but causes the skin around his right eye to crease just slightly. His eyes are piercing, a pale blue that looks oddly out of place against his tan complexion and dark hair.

"Alex," I say, trying to stay cool. This is the third time in as many days I've introduced myself as *Alex*. It just seems right somehow.

"Where are you from, Alex?"

Oh. I like the way he said my name. His lips curl around the syllables like a particularly delicious fruit, and it makes goosebumps run down the back of my neck.

"I'm from San Francisco," I reply, trying to keep my breathing under control.

He smiles, a quirky smile. It makes me want to smile back. Truth be told, it makes me want to do a lot more than smile. "Really? I'm from Atlanta. Never been out West."

I struggle for something to say. "It's my first trip East by myself," I said.

He settles in, stuffing his bag under the seat in front of him. He takes a small blister pack out of his pocket and peels it back, then pops a square object in his mouth. It doesn't look like a pill. More like gum, really. Nicotine gum? Crank tried to quit smoking last year and chewed the stuff constantly.

Dylan says in his soft Southern accent, "Tell me about yourself, Alex."

By this time, the captain is speaking, and the flight attendant begins walking up and down the aisles checking seats as the plane departs from the gate.

I sit back, unsure what to say. He put me on the spot, and I have no idea what to say. *I'm Alex, and all I do is study. I don't have a life really, except barely reflecting my much more brilliant and colorful sisters.* Instead, I say, "That's a pretty open-ended question."

His face flushes a little. Then he says, with a twinkle in his eye and a funny looking grin on his face, "I guess. Let me start over. I'm Dylan, and I have lousy social skills. I'd like to get to know you by asking stupid questions. How's that?"

I burst into laughter, and he laughs too, and everything is okay. "Tell you what," I say. "I'll ask you a question, then you ask me a question, then I'll ask you a question."

As I speak, his grin grows larger. "They have to be specific questions. And you can't lie."

He makes a mock wounded face. "Do I look like someone who would lie?"

I laugh. "Silly, your questions are supposed to be about me, not you."

For the next two hours, we throw questions back and forth. This is challenging. He opens simply. *Do I ever ride on the street cars in San Francisco?* But then it turns more serious. I ask him, "What scares you more than anything else in the world?"

His answer stuns me, mostly because it *isn't* superficial. He says, "Ending up like my dad. He was a drunk."

Jesus. I try to change the subject. He's worried about turning out like his Dad—everybody *wants* me to be like mine. Even though technically it isn't my turn to ask a question, I do anyway. "What's the best thing you've ever done?"

He thinks it over, his eyebrows shoved together almost comically, then he replies with something I never anticipated. "I was homeless for a while. Dropped out of school. Anyway, sometimes I didn't know where I was going to sleep, or get something to eat. One night I was riding on MARTA... that's our subway... just back and forth, trying to get some sleep on the train before they shut down for the night. They shut down the train at 2 a.m., and I was stuck downtown, and I ran into a family. All of them were homeless, like me. Parents, two kids. The dad had lost his job . And I was working, doing some landscaping and day labor, so I had a little bit of money. So I treated them to dinner at Waffle House. It wasn't much... maybe twenty dollars. But you could tell the kids hadn't been eating much at all. They were so... grateful."

I'm speechless. *Homeless?* I'm honestly not sure I can even believe him, except that he doesn't come across as a liar. "You were homeless?"

"No, that's an extra question. My turn. Why do you smell like strawberries?"

My face turns red hot. "Umm..." I said, because that was as coherent a thought as I could put together. "I ... um... it's my shampoo. I like strawberries... I wear strawberry lip gloss, too."

Now *he* blushes. That makes me smile, because where I come from, guys don't blush. But this one does, and I like it. A lot. We talk about other things. He's dating a girl—casually, he says, not serious—and I'm dating a guy too. Also not serious. Then we veer from that to other subjects, because really who wants to spend all this time talking about people who aren't even here?

***

"What's your favorite book?" he asks me.

"The Unbearable Lightness of Being."

His face makes a comical expression. "Please, clarify."

I laugh. Then I find myself trying to explain why this novel of 1968 Prague captured my mind so. "Love is fleeting. Random. Coincidence? I don't know how to explain, exactly."

"You don't believe we're fated to have someone we love?" His eyes seem to be focused straight into my heart as he asks the question..

I look back at him, refusing to give into the weight of his question. "I don't," I reply. "I mean, look at my parents. Random. My Dad walked into a flower shop in Barcelona of all places and met my mother. If he'd never walked into that shop—or if he'd walked into a different one—everything would have been different. If they hadn't fallen in love, everything would have been different. I wouldn't even be alive."

Dylan smiles. "Maybe it was fated to be."

I shrug. "I don't know about all that."

"Sisters," he says. "How many sisters are we talking?"

"Five."

As always, stunned silence and raised eyebrows. "There are five of you?"

I laugh. "Not five of *me*. We're all different. And it's a total of six."

"Wow. Are you the oldest? Youngest?"

"I'm exactly in the middle," I reply. "Julia and Carrie are in their twenties—Carrie's in graduate school at

Columbia. I turn seventeen next week, and I have three younger sisters. You?"

"No siblings. And I'm eighteen. And happy birthday." Dylan smiles as he says the words *happy birthday*.

"You're a senior, then."

He nods.

"Where are you planning to go to college?" I ask.

He shrugs. I sit back. "You don't know? But you're in your senior year... what about your applications? They should be in by now, you'll hardly have time in December when we get back."

He grimaces. "Well... to be honest, I was planning to take a year or two off. I want to travel."

"Travel? Where?"

He smiles. "South Asia, maybe. India, or possibly Vietnam?"

"But... why?" I'm genuinely puzzled. I've lived all over the globe. I can't see any reason to just *travel* if it means not going to college.

"Well... I'm going to be a writer. And while I could learn a lot in college, I'll learn more on the road. If I really want to be writing, I need to be experiencing life."

I don't laugh. But I do say, "That's the craziest thing I've ever heard."

He shrugs, then gives me that sideways grin. That *maddening* sideways grin.

Who consciously decides they aren't going to college? I don't understand him.

Alex Thompson's eyes (Dylan)

Every step of the way through this conversation, I wonder if I'm screwing up. When I told her I'd been homeless, her eyes widened so much I thought they were going to fall out. Same when I told her I had no plans for college. After all, *all* of the kids on this trip have plans in place for their lives.

Sometimes I feel like I had no map. And that's just highlighted all the more in the presence of so much drive and direction.

Look, I get it. When you're a senior in high school, you're supposed to be thinking about graduation, and college, and grad school, and what your career is going to be. But really, it's kind of chancy whether or not I'll even graduate. I mean—I dropped out when I was sixteen. I've been busting my ass to catch up with my class. One screw-up, one bad grade, and I could lose it. Being here? It doesn't seem real.

I think part of me thinks I'll end up back under that bridge some day. That I'll end up on drugs again, or drinking again.

That I'll end up like Dad.

I've got people who believe in me. Mom. Mister Philler, my principal. They stood behind me and pushed and helped every step of the way. They've encouraged me to apply to college—Mom to Georgia State, and Mister Philler has been pushing me to apply to other, more selective colleges, too. But I've made it very clear to everyone who asks what my plans are. Experience first. Then college. This foreign exchange trip—which

I never imagined I'd actually be selected for—is just the first step.

It's really kind of interesting, the groups of students on this trip. Each of a dozen or so cities sent five kids, and they all had their own criteria for selecting the students who attended. In Atlanta, we went through a nomination and application process, essays and an oral presentation. The kids from Atlanta are all over the economic spectrum—Tameka's family owns a small chain of hotels, Naila's family is getting food stamps. Some of the other cities aren't as varied. All of the kids in the Washington, DC delegation come from the same high school, a public school but only marginally so, located in the upper northwest amongst two-million dollar homes.

But one thing they all have in common? They know where they are going.

I need somewhere to steer the conversation. Not my parents, my homelessness, or my aimlessness. So I start to ask her questions. What is her school like? How did she like Moscow? Where else has she lived? What is it like being the child of an ambassador?

She answers all of them, but asks some of her own. And with every pause in the conversation, every time I look her in the eyes, I fall a little deeper.

Let me tell you about Alex Thompson's eyes.

First, her eyes and her face are framed by long brown hair. Not dark, but a more vibrant brown with slightly red and blonde highlights. Her skin is olive, with full lips and high cheek bones. Lips to linger over. Her mother's Spanish heritage is obvious. Highly arched eyebrows, and a straight, perfectly-sized nose. Her eyes are green, beautifully spaced, and full. They are eyes to get lost in.

But it's not just her eyes. It's what's behind them. For an almost-seventeen-year-old, she's remarkably experienced with life. I don't see that with my friends at school back home. She's lived in a bunch of different places, all over the world. She speaks a lot of Russian and some Chinese. Crazy. But that's not all. Behind all that, when she talks about her family? There's some sadness lurking there. I want to know what is all about.

I realized as we talk and talk during that flight that I want her very badly. But there are two *very* big problems.

First—she is so far out of my league it isn't even funny. I'm the kid of a drunk, I've been homeless, I have no plans for college. She is the wealthy child of a U.S. Ambassador and headed to Harvard or Columbia. She's going to turn down colleges, not the other way around.

Second—this little jaunt around the world will be over in five weeks. Thirty-four days, then we'll return to our own little corners of the world, and that will be it. As I get lost in her eyes, that's all I can remember. I could so easily fall in love with this girl.

But, on the thirty-fourth day, I will lose her.

CHAPTER FOUR

Let me see your eyes (Dylan)

THE KNOCK ON the door is followed by the appearance of John, one of my new bunkmates, who opens it and sticks his head in, his short, extremely curly hair still wet from the shower.

"Yo, Mike, Dylan," he barks, loud enough I'm startled. "Let's head into town."

I look up. I'm laying on my bunk in the Tel Aviv Youth Hostel, splayed out and resting. My bag, which finally caught up with me this morning, is open on the floor next to me. We spent the day on a tour bus, going from a museum in the morning to a school in the afternoon, followed by a brief bus tour of the Old City of Jaffa. I was disappointed we couldn't get off the bus then, because it looked fascinating, and far more ancient than modern Tel Aviv.

Unfortunately, we were whisked back to the hostel for dinner. But now, we've been released to our own devices. I sit up. "What are your plans?"

John shrugs. "Walk down the street and see what we see."

"Let's go," says Mike, who currently sits across the room from me, his arms and legs stretched out comically on the one chair in the room.

"I'm in," I reply. "Who else is going along?"

"You know Elle?"

I shake my head.

John waggles his eyebrows and makes a scrunching motion with his hands that leaves little room for mistake about what he thinks of her appearance. "*That* Elle. She's from New York. Her roommates are coming too. Not sure who they are."

John is crude. But I have to admit, it doesn't hurt my eyes when I look at Elle. A few minutes later I've changed, we've gathered our things and we're on our way out the door.

In the lobby, we meet up with the girls. I nod toward Alex and casually say, "Hey." I don't trust myself to say much more than that. Seeing her fills me with desire and anxiety and attraction and more than a little bit of lust. I barely know her, and she barely knows me, and even if we did know each other, we're only here for a few weeks.

So I keep my distance. Instead, I walk along next to John, who I only met as we were getting situated in our rooms last night.

John Modesta is from Long Island, New York. He's brash, quick with words, a little loud, a little obnoxious. I've never spent so much time around people from cities up north. But he's not rude. In fact just the opposite—he's been one of the friendlier people I've met thus far on this trip. I'll be the first to admit I'm not the most outgoing person on earth—I like people all right, but I've never gone out of my way to make friends. And my background is very different from most of them.

I keep pace with him while he launches into a lengthy monologue. He starts by talking about the differences between New York and Tel Aviv (at least the half a dozen square blocks of Tel Aviv which we've seen so far). New York is dirtier, more crowded, busier. But it's also more interesting, livelier and more artsy. He then moves on to the comparative smells (New York smells much worse, he claims, describing the smell as "dead bodies" versus the smell of rotting garbage in Tel Aviv).

The street we walk on—Dizengoff Street—is lined with sidewalk cafes, open restaurants and stores and far more. But it doesn't have the look and feel of a tourist area like some of the part of New York I saw during our brief stay there. Just the opposite, really. The cafes are lined with people, out in large numbers with friends and family. I hear laughter and see a lot of people of all ages.

Along both sides of the street are signs, primarily in English and Hebrew, but a smattering in other languages—French, some Arabic, other European languages I would guess might be German and Spanish. The signs are colorful and modern looking.

Alex Thompson walks along talking with Elle LaDuke, a girl from the New York delegation. Elle, the object of John's crude affection, is petite, with shoulder length black hair, all black clothes and very pale face. The only spot of color on her is her eyes (blue) and her lips (painted bright red). I can hear her questioning Alex—where does she go to school? What did she think of New York? Elle's voice has a world-weary weight to it, like a jaded, experienced traveller coaching along a much younger friend. I keep an ear open to their conversation as Elle begins to talk about the week she spent in Paris her freshman year in high school.

"It was really duller than I thought it would be," she says. "And the hotel accommodations were disappointing. But really, nothing helps one become more—cultured—than travel. I'm sure you'll feel much the same after this trip."

Alex's eyes cut over to me. I can almost hear her screaming inside. I chime in, "Alex told me she felt the same about Moscow, that it was much less interesting than when she lived in China."

"Only because of the snow," Alex says. "Moscow is really cold in the winter time."

"Oh," Elle says. "You've been to Moscow?"

"Yes, but our stay was cut short, we were only there for a year."

"And China?"

"Three years in Beijing. I was pretty young, though; I don't remember as much as I would like."

Elle swallows. Her face is actually flushed red. I say, "Alex's father was a U.S. Ambassador, so she travelled a lot."

That silences Elle. Actually, it silences the whole group.

So I say, "I, on the other hand, have never been anywhere, except one week in Destin, Florida. Outside of that, this is my first trip out of Georgia." I don't know why I said it. Except it was an uncomfortable moment for everyone, and guess I felt like I needed to rescue the situation.

"Really?" John says. "I wouldn't have guessed. I assumed a Georgia native might be a little more... backward."

"Oh yeah?" I say. Maybe I'm too sensitive, but Elle and John both ... I really want them to shut up. I half-expected this—let's be honest, sometimes people are idiots. Just a little. But what the hell? In for a penny, in for a pound. "Was it the Klan hood that threw you off, or maybe the lack of shoes?"

John stops in his tracks. "I didn't mean to say—"

I reply, "You didn't mean to say... what?"

He shakes his head. "Sorry man. I didn't mean to be an asshole."

"Yeah," Elle says. "Me neither."

"It's okay," I say almost at the exact same time Alex says, "Don't worry about it."

"What do you say we stop and grab a drink?" John says. "I feel bad now."

"We should just get wasted," Mike from Chicago finally chimes in, his first contribution to the night's conversation. He's so gangly I bet it only takes half a beer to get him drunk.

"I'm all for some coffee," I say, "but I don't drink. Don't let me stop you, though."

They all look at me like I just said that I live on Mars. Then they move on, as if I hadn't even said it. "I heard there's no problem getting served here," John says.

"Getting drunk is probably ill-advised," Elle says. "I don't think the program would like it."

"Whatever." John shrugs.

"Wait, what's that?" Alex asks. She's pointing down the side street. In the distance, the street just comes to an end... the beach, apparently. Off to one side, a lighthouse.

"Jaffa," Alex says. Unlike modern Tel Aviv, Jaffa has buildings which are hundreds, some of them thousands, of years old. Without anyone saying a word, we all turn toward the side street and the buildings ahead. A hush falls over the group—for a few seconds—but that is broken when John cracks a joke and the girls laugh. I don't catch the joke, whatever it was, but not knowing the content makes me feel uncomfortable. Like they're laughing at me.

Realistically, I know they aren't. It doesn't make any sense. They don't know anything about me. But every time I see their expensive sweaters and boots, their phones and gadgets, I know I am different. After all, it hadn't been *that* long since I'd been a dropout living on the streets.

We are getting close to the water now. I can smell it, a strange smell, salt and something else I can't quite pin down. I'd never been to the ocean before my week in Destin last year. This is all unfamiliar territory for me.

Especially the girl who approaches me as we reached the water.

Alex Thompson.

She has her arms crossed over her chest, and I ask her, automatically, "Are you cold? Can I give you my jacket?" I don't have much of a jacket on me, just a light-weight windbreaker, but it's better than nothing.

"No, thanks," she says. "I'm okay."

"Look at this!" John shouts, gesturing at the surf. He let out a "whoop!" as he runs for the pier that leads far out into the Mediterranean. Mike and Elle and the other girl, who hasn't been introduced, follow.

Alex sits down on the stone wall and looks out. I drop onto the wall next to her.

She speaks in a steady, inquisitive tone, "I'd pay a million dollars to know what you've been thinking about the last few minutes," she says.

Heck, she probably could. I try not to think about that. "My thoughts the last few minutes haven't been worth a million dollars. Wait a while, and I'll let you know when I can make that worth your while."

She lets out a low laugh. "Two shekels, then."

"Well, in that case," I say, after I finish calculating the exchange rate, "I was thinking that I'm not like everyone here. That I don't belong here."

"Why not? Because you used to be homeless?"

I nod, once. "That, as much as anything."

She shrugs. "I think that makes you better qualified than most of us on this trip."

I grunt, because I have nothing to say to that.

"Tell me your favorite color," she says.

"Green," I reply.

"Any particular shade?"

I say, "Let me see your eyes."

Even though it's dark, I can still see her skin flush in the street light. See, I *can* do some things right. I feel a little light-headed as I say the next words: "That color."

She shakes her head and looks out toward the water. There is an awkward pause. "What about politics? You a Democrat? Republican?"

I shrug. "It's all bullshit if you're poor. Both sides want you to vote for them, but poor people are too tired and stressed to learn about politics."

"You sound like you know something about it."

I smile grimly. "I generally like the way the Democrats treat people and the way the Republicans treat defense."

"You think invading Iraq was right?"

I shrug. "Given the information we had at the time, sure."

"What about... gay people? Do you think they should marry?"

I chuckle. "I could care less if they marry or not. I'm not gay, it don't mean a hill of beans to me."

She nods. "What about here? The Israeli-Palestinian conflict."

"Well, it seems like most of our friends here are committed Zionists."

Her mouth twists up on one side. "See—you keep saying you don't belong here, like you aren't as smart as these people. I bet most of them don't even know what a Zionist is."

"It's a damn shame," I say, "since most of them will go on to be the kinds of people who decide what our country does. Don't you think that's sad?"

She smiles. "I do. Though I know a lot of people involved with our foreign policy. People like my dad. He knows his stuff—he works hard, and he cares about doing the right thing."

I shrug. "My dad's probably in jail."

She slaps me on the shoulder. "So what *do* you think about this place?"

I shake my head. "Hell, I don't know. It's too early. I've read a few books—fiction. Leon Uris and Amos Oz. Susan Abulhawa. Just because I was curious what I was getting into."

"I know about Leon Uris," she says. "Who are the others?"

I raise an eyebrow. "Amos Oz is Israel's leading novelist. He's really good. Abulhawa wrote *Mornings in Jenin*. It's brilliant… follows a refugee family through four generations."

She smiles. "I'd bet you're the only student on this trip who has read this much."

I shrug. "Maybe. There's no point in coming all this way if I'm not ready to learn something. This is a once in a lifetime opportunity. I'm not gonna waste it. Plus … I want to be a writer. You don't get to be good at that without paying attention."

She arches an eyebrow. "Your reading doesn't give you any conclusions?"

"Not yet. What about you?"

"Well, my father would say that Israel has a right to defend itself. That it's a tiny state surrounded by enemies."

"That's pretty much what everyone's been saying since we got here."

"What do you like to do in your free time, Dylan?"

"Write stories. And the occasional poem. What about you?"

"I play violin some. Not as well as my sister Julia, though. She's really good. And... I like to think about the future. I read about interesting things. I want to do interesting things."

"What sort of things?"

"I'm planning to go to law school. I want to work for the ACLU or Amnesty International. I want to help people who need it."

Now I smile at her. "What does your father think of that goal? Didn't you say he was a bigwig with the Republicans?"

"Not really. He's big with the government, and got himself involved in McCain's campaign. But really, he doesn't get into electoral politics that much. Though he *is* super conservative."

"It's good to have a little rebellion," I say.

"Do you rebel against your parents—I mean, your mom?"

I quickly shake my head. "That's all over with for me. Mom's my biggest cheerleader and ally."

She take a deep, shuddering breath. "I envy you for that."

"What about you?"

She shrugs. "My mother's a little crazy, if you want to know the truth. The only thing that makes her tolerable is the meds she takes to keep her anxiety and emotional fuckery under control."

Emotional fuckery. There's a term. I want to write that down somewhere. She continues, unaware that I'm admiring her phrasing. "That's basically it. Dad's gone all the time—I haven't seen him in months. Mom's a basket case. With my older sisters gone, that leaves me to fend for myself and protect the twins."

I do some math in my head. She's mentioned two older sisters, and two younger twins. "Didn't you say you had three younger sisters?"

She nods. "Yes. Andrea—she's the youngest—lives with our grandmother, in Spain."

"Really? Why?"

She shakes her head sadly. "That's the million dollar question. None of us know. I guess Mom and Dad do, but they aren't telling anybody."

"Weird," I say.

"Yeah," she responds glumly.

Time for a change of subject. "Have you heard any details about your host family?"

She shakes her head. "Just a name. Ariel Jabarin."

"Same here. Nothing but a name. Dari Peretz."

"We'll find out soon enough," she says.

I nod. In the morning, we meet our host families for the first third of the exchange program. I'm not really looking forward to that. See, when I was in between homes, I spent a lot of time couchsurfing. I'd stay with one friend for a few days, then another. I'd crash in a basement, or on a sofa. The one thing I never had during that period was my own place. Even if it's only for a few weeks, the idea of going back to being a guest all the time is difficult to get my mind around. But I don't really have any choice.

She says, "Will you let me know how it goes?"

"Of course," I say. "I don't know how…" I trail off.

"Facebook, silly."

"Is that kind of like MySpace?"

She nods, but sort of winces at the same time. "Yes, but not as obnoxious."

"Oh, perfect. I don't have an account, on MySpace or Facebook. But I guess I can set one up if I can get to a computer."

"How about you set one up when we get back to the hostel."

"Okay…." My voice trails off again. She says it casually. I know there are a couple of computers in the common room. But I've never done social networking of any kind.

A cynical thought passes through my head. I wonder if Spot has a MySpace account. I bet she does, and I bet if I had one, I'd know where she is today. More enthusiastically, I say, "Yeah. I'll set it up tonight."

"And I get to be your first friend," she says. The smile on her face shows a row of broad, white teeth. It's hard for me to pull my eyes away from her.

Hours pass before we decide to head back to the hostel. At one point Elle says, "Well, you two sure are getting along." But she says little else.

Technically our curfew was ten p.m.—it's almost that late now. But as we walk back up the street, along the outskirts of the Old City, I see what looks like an ancient stone building. It's dark, with nothing but holes where the window and doors should be. I stop, trying to see in. Most of the building doesn't even have a roof.

"Let's check it out," I say.

"No way, man," John says. "Place looks like it would collapse around you."

Mike shakes his head.

I frown. "Come on, it's just a building. It looks ancient."

They look at me like I'm crazy. I shrug. Then Alex says, "I'll come with you."

Instantly I feel a rush of emotion. Because after the others refused, I was hoping she would say that. I grin and invite her in.

I step forward, and through the arched opening. It's dark in here, but I can see light from the moon, and a little from the streetlamp, flooding through a hole in the roof. Alex steps in beside me. I can feel her presence in the dark next to me.

"What are we doing?" she whispers.

"I don't know... exploring?" I respond in the same whisper. I don't know why. But I take a slow step forward, and she stays beside me. Beyond the front room, there's a small hallway. Everything is dusty stone, undoubtedly tan.

"This place is really old," she whispers.

From the door, John or Mike slowly makes a mournful wolf-howl.

"Asshole," Alex calls back to them. Then she grabs my hand. I suck in a quick breath. Her hand touching mine has a weight all its own. We keep walking forward.

"Watch your step," I say. It looks like steps leading down, not far. Then we pass through another archway, and we're in a courtyard.

The courtyard is lit only by the moon, but it's lit well enough to tell that it was once a garden. Now, it's overgrown with vines and bushes, flowers everywhere. The fragrance is overwhelming.

"Oh my God, it's beautiful," she whispers.

"Yeah," I say. I squeeze her hand, then both of us let our hands drop, like we'd been stung by bees.

We only stay for two or three minutes. From the street, Elle calls, "Alex? You okay?"

"Yes!" Alex responds. "Be right out."

She sighs after a minute. "I don't want to leave," she says. "It's magical."

I smile at her, though she probably can't see that well. Five minutes later, we get back out to the street. John says, "What was in there?"

"Nothing," Alex says, apparently wanting the same thing I so, to keep the courtyard a secret. "Just dust."

Our eyes meet, and she gives me a faint smile, and we continue on our way.

Wasn't Jewish Enough (Alex)

The next morning, we gather for breakfast in the main room of the hostel. Coffee, toast, Nutella. I sit with John and Mike, Elle and Dylan, and I find myself laughing and enjoying myself. Dylan does a passable imitation of President Bush, which keeps us all laughing through breakfast.

I don't mention to Dylan, or anyone else, that I've met George Bush and eaten at the White House. I already feel alien enough. And I'm still mentally out of breath from last night and our adventure in the abandoned building. I don't know how old it was, but it *felt* ancient, and the courtyard was like something out of a fairy tale.

I grabbed Dylan's hand automatically. I felt ... safe with him, even in a dark and abandoned building. Crazy, I know. But something about his confidence made me feel completely comfortable walking through there, and *that* made it magical finding that courtyard.

As breakfast is finished, the tour organizers stand up to give more speeches and information. We'll be breaking apart into three groups—one group headed to Haifa, the other to Jerusalem, and the final one staying here in Tel Aviv. After 8 days, we'll rotate, so each group spends about a week in each of the three cities.

I feel a momentary panic that I'm to be separated from Dylan. And that scares me. First, because we aren't anything. We aren't dating, we aren't a couple, we aren't in love, we aren't *anything*. Second, because even if we were any of those things, well, this whole trip comes to an end in just a few weeks. I need to get a serious grip. Plus, I still haven't gotten around to writing Mike. Mike, whom I'm supposedly dating, even if it has only been a couple of dinners.

After breakfast, we separate into our groups, and I'm relieved to see that Dylan is in my group. It's time to meet our host families.

A few minutes later, I find myself faced with a couple in their fifties and their teenage son.

Teenage *son*. He has blonde sculpted hair, muscular upper arms and a five-o-clock shadow.

"I'm Ariel," he says.

I cough. "I'm Alex."

He grins. I look at his parents. Would it be wrong of me to ask where their daughter is?

I look back. "It's nice to meet you, Ariel. Excuse me for a moment."

I walk directly over to Marie Simpson, one of the chaperone's from San Francisco. She looks stressed. Why the hell would I get placed with a guy? Did they get our names mixed up? Maybe someone on this end though *Alex* was a guy's name, or *Ariel* a girl's. I don't know.

"Excuse me, Mrs. Simpson."

"Yes, Alex?"

"Um… I'm confused… Ariel… my host student? It's a guy."

She frowns. "That can't be right," she says. "Are you sure?"

"Um… yeah. I'm sure. It's pretty unmistakable."

She closes her eyes and rubs a hand on her forehead. "That sounds like a mixup. You're supposed to be staying with a girl, of course."

"That's what I thought," I say.

"We don't have any more host families," she says.

I lean closer and say, "Maybe there's a guy in our group who was put with a girl? Maybe we got switched?"

She looks like she isn't sure what to say. And I'm certainly not sure. She finally settles on, "I'll check. In the meantime, go with your host family, and we'll get back with you today."

I swallow, then glance over my shoulder. Ariel is standing there, practically salivating. I don't know him yet, but I already want to punch him in the throat. Probably not the ideal start. "Are you sure?" I ask. "This isn't what I expected."

Mrs. Simpson puts her hands on my shoulders and looks me in the eyes. "Alex... we'll take care of it. I promise."

I sighed. Nothing else to be done. I walked back to the waiting family. "Sorry about that," I say. "It's all set."

"Do you have all of your bags?" the mother says. "I'm Rebecca. This is my husband Josef"

Rebecca's English is as good as mine—possibly better. She holds out her hand to shake—I take it. Maybe this won't be so bad.

"It's nice to meet you all," I say.

"And you, young lady," Josef says. Unlike his wife, he has a strong eastern European accent. "Is there anything you need before we go?"

I shake my head no. On second thought, it's a Russian accent. But if Rebecca isn't from the midwest, I would be shocked. Josef picks up one of my bags, and I reach for the other, but Josef says, "No, Ariel. Take the young lady's bag."

Ariel flashes me an unreadable look. Then he picks up my bag. I search around the area. Dylan is getting into a car about a hundred yards away. He sees me and his face brightens into a smile. He waves.

I wave back, trying not to show my worry. Swallowing, I follow Rebecca down the street to a perfect-condition, bright-blue Mitsubishi. Josef opens the trunk—it looks as if it has never been used. Perfectly clean carpet inside; not a speck of dust. The four of us get into the car, Josef and Rebecca in front, Ariel and myself in back. Ariel twists in his seat and openly stares at me, but his mother says something in a sharp tone in Hebrew. He turns his eyes to the front and buckles up.

"Is Alex short for Alexandra?" Josef asks.

"Yes," I reply.

"My mother was an Alexandra. It seems a pity to shorten a beautiful name."

I shrug, then make use of my very limited Russian to ask him if he is from Russia. "Вы из России?"

His face erupts into a huge smile. "Changing the subject, I see. Da—I'm originally from Saint Petersburg. I moved to Israel in 1991 with my parents. I'm surprised you can distinguish the accent?"

"My family lived in Moscow for a year when I was younger. But that's just about all the Russian I remember."

"I see!" Josef replies.

"Where do you live now?" Rebecca asks.

"San Francisco."

"Beautiful city."

I look at her. "Where are you from?"

"Minneapolis, actually."

Ariel interrupts. "I was born in Tel Aviv."

Josef pulls the car into the heavy traffic along Dizengoff Street, but soon turns off, getting out of the traffic by maneuvering through a bewildering set of twists and turns.

"How did you end up in Israel?" I ask.

Josef says, "You know about when Soviet Union collapsed? My parents moved here then—about a million Russian Jews come to Israel then."

A million? This is a tiny country. "I had no idea."

Rebecca smiles. "I came here a couple years after that. I was an idealistic girl."

"Now, not so much," Josef comments.

She frowns at him. "Speak for yourself, husband."

He chuckles. "I always speak for myself, wife."

I can't help but smile at how they refer to each other. The couple begins a lighthearted debate about who is more cynical, and then as the discussion becomes more passionate and animated, they lapse into Hebrew.

I comment quietly to Ariel, "I like how they call each other *husband* and *wife.*"

Ariel says, "They do that because they only just got married last year."

"Really?" I'm a little shocked, though I ought not be.

Josef overheard the exchange and lets out a loud, bark like laugh. "It's because even though we were so Jewish the Russians hated us, I wasn't Jewish *enough* for the Rabbis here."

I am a little confused.

Rebecca says, "In Israel, marriage has to be approved by the religious authorities. Josef couldn't prove his mother was Jewish, so they wouldn't let him marry me. We held out for years, hoping they would do the right thing, but finally decided to get married in Minneapolis. The government recognizes marriages conducted in other countries."

"That makes no sense," I say. "How do you prove you are Jewish?"

"The birth certificate has to note that the mother was a Jew. And you have to be able to prove you were circumcised as a baby."

"Huh," I say. Josef steers the car onto a highway. Traffic is awful.

"We live in Ramat Gan," Josef says, "If you are curious."

"Where is Ramat Gan?" I ask.

"It's a suburb to the east of Tel Aviv," Josef replies. "You will like it. All of the host families for your program are in Ramat Gan. You'll see all of your friends tomorrow morning at the high school."

I sigh with some relief. I've got phone numbers for our chaperones, of course, as well as the program headquarters. I'm glad I'll be seeing everyone in the morning.

"In the meantime," Rebecca says, "we have big dinner plans. Josef's parents and brother will be coming over for dinner. You'll love them."

I struggle to maintain an enthusiastic smile, because that's what my mother trained me to do. But inside, I'm almost crying. I've reached my fill of people for the day, though it's only ten in the morning. I'm on my way to who knows where, and I didn't realize until I got into this car just how much I've taken it for granted that my host student would be another girl. It's not that I feel unsafe, but... I've never had any brothers.

I look over at Ariel. Why did they have to screw up my placement?

CHAPTER FIVE

Leave her alone (Dylan)

"I DARE YOU. You have a beer. I pay."

I close my eyes. Rami might be Dari's best friend, but he's also a giant dick. I look at Dari, my host-student. He's oblivious, his eyes glued on Elle, who is dressed, tonight, in a flared mid-thigh length skirt and a skin-tight white tank which shows an exceptional amount of cleavage. It's hard to blame him, really, though I've drifted from indifference to Elle over the last few days to genuine dislike. She's superficial, self-absorbed and generally an all-around bitch, but it's also a fact that she's easy on the eyes.

So Dari is no help. I turn back to Rami. "Listen— Rami. Thanks for offering, but I don't drink. I'll just have a coffee."

A moment later, Alex storms into the pub. Her face is set with an angry expression, lips compressed, a fierce line between her eyebrows. I stand up as she approaches. "You okay?"

She nods. "Can I sit with you?"

I wave to the seat next to me—one of the only two empty seats left at the table. It's our third day in Ramat Gan, and our host students had gotten together and agreed to meet here at the Boston Brewery and Pub. The decor in the bar seems to be loosely based on the bar in the TV show *Cheers,* which is still syndicated in

Israel. Alex drops into the seat just as the door to the pub opens.

Ariel, her host student, marches in. He looks frustrated. Ariel is little more than a large ball of glands and hormones dressed in modern clothing, so I have few doubts what he's frustrated about. And that makes me want to pound him into a very *tiny* ball of hormones.

I lean close to Alex and whisper. "Is he still bothering you?"

She frowns. Then nods, her lips set in a bitter line.

The waitress arrives and begins taking orders. Rami orders a beer for me. I interrupt and say, "Just coffee for me, thanks." The waitress continues taking down the order, then steps away.

I whisper, "What did Mrs. Simpson say?"

"They haven't settled on a host family yet." Her eyes are a little wet.

"Maybe you should call your father."

Her eyes meet mine. In a firm voice, she says, "I'd rather sleep on the street."

I snort. "You have no idea what you're talking about."

"Neither do you," she responds. "You don't show weakness with my parents, or they'll use it to twist a knife."

Jesus. Ariel approaches the end of the table, where Alex is seated and stands facing her, looking down. He's breathing heavily, and his face is red.

"Leave me alone, Ariel."

"I didn't mean it, Alex."

Didn't mean what?

"I said, leave me alone."

He leans toward her, hands gripping the table. His angle above her is intimidating. "Alex, listen to me."

"We're done here," she says.

"We're *not* done."

I stand up. I don't think about it. I just back away from the table and walk around it toward Ariel. He's taller than I am, and heavier, more muscular. But he's also an idiot. My heart is beating rapidly, too rapidly. I'm moving too quickly to think, too quickly to realize I'm afraid.

"Dylan, stop," Alex says. "I don't need—"

I come to a stop in front of Ariel, whose attention is now fully on me. I poke him in the chest with a finger and say, "You heard her. Leave her alone."

He looks at me astonished. This close up, he's *really* tall. Taller than six feet. And his upper arms look like small tree trunks. He works out. "Get out of my way *fri'er,* if you want to live."

I stare up at him. I don't know what *fri'er* means, but it's probably not good. "Work it out, asshole. How's it going to look for you if you get kicked out of this program because of sexual harassment. Huh? You're smarter than that."

Dari, attention finally yanked away from Elle, mutters, "I doubt that." But the good news is, he stands and comes around the table next to me. Dari is as thin as one of his drumsticks, but it's still helpful to have him beside me against another Israeli.

Rami stands as well. He walks up behind Ariel and stands on his tip-toes (Rami is easily the shortest person in the room) and stage-whispers something in Hebrew. I don't know what it is, but it convinces Ariel. He sags a little, as if someone had pricked a balloon. Then he turns and walks out of the pub.

Then Rami says, "Cheers for Dylan, eh?" Everyone at the table suddenly claps, except Alex. "Now I *have* to buy you a drink."

With an exasperated growl, I say, "I don't drink, Rami! Let it alone!"

I return to my seat.

Alex doesn't say anything. She just stares forward.

I frown. I wasn't expecting her to jump at me or to throw flowers at me as if I were her champion or something, but a simple *thanks* might have been nice. What the hell? Instead, she's sitting there, not looking at me, not saying anything. She looks *angry*.

Then she stands. And walks to the door and out.

What. The. Hell?

I jump to my feet. "Excuse me, guys; I'll be back."

The door bangs open as I get out onto the street. This is a crappy little street, lined with fast-food joints and a few electronics and convenience stores. Alex is already fifty feet away and moving at a fast pace. *Where does she think she's going?*

"Hey! Alex!"

She doesn't stop. *Christ on a crutch*. I run after her.

"Where are you going?" I ask when I finally catch up.

"Back to my host family, of course. Where else am I going to go?" She's almost in tears.

"What the hell, Alex? What did I do wrong?"

She stops and turns toward me. "What did you do wrong? More like, what did you do right? You don't own me, Dylan Paris. You don't even really know me. We aren't dating. We aren't *anything.*"

I want to say: we could be. But I don't. Instead, I say, "I was just trying to help."

"You can help by listening," she says. Then her eyes cut to our left, and she mutters something. Our compatriots are approaching: Dari and Rami, Elle and John and Mike.

Rami announces, with a shout, "Party at my place. 9 o'clock Friday. Be there!"

He's not a bad boy (Alex)

Despite my anger, Dylan insists on walking me back to Ariel's. Which means, of course, that Dari, his host student, also tags along. Dari is gangly, with close-cut dark curly hair and a face covered in a mess of freckles and dark brown eyes. Behind him trails his best friend Rami. Rami isn't hosting a student, but runs in the same circles as most of the kids who are. Honestly, I'm liking *all* of them less and less each day I've been here. Ariel, especially.

We finally arrive outside the apartment building. Josef and Rebecca's car is parked underneath the building—good news, since I wasn't going in if they weren't home. I'm not looking forward to the conversation I'm about to have.

"Okay. This is where I go up alone."

Dylan looks concerned. "Are you sure?"

"Yes. Look, Ariel's parents are home, their car is right there."

"If he touches you…"

"Dylan. Shut up. First of all, he hasn't, and won't. Ariel is a giant dick, but he's all words and looks. I'm going to talk with his parents, then with Mrs. Simpson, and then Mrs. Simpson is going to find me a new place to sleep. The end. Okay?"

He swallows. I can see the tension in his body, his upper arms slightly flexed, his feet almost shoulder width apart. He looks like he's ready to find Ariel and beat the crap out of him right this minute.

No one needs that. Especially not Dylan, who would be in all kinds of trouble if he got in a fight. I ought to be annoyed. I'm perfectly capable of taking care of myself. I don't need some hyped-up, testosterone-filled guy to protect me.

"Okay," he says. Then he blurts out, "Sorry," almost as if he really means it.

He doesn't move. It's awkward, but I turn away, cross the street, and enter the apartment building.

Ariel and his family live on the second floor. I don't know what standards people in Israel are used to, but to me, it seems *very* cramped. But I live in a four-story Victorian in San Francisco, and even when we lived in Washington we were in a large six-bedroom condominium. Josef and Rebecca rent an apartment that maybe has six hundred square feet centered around a combined living area and dining room. They were just as surprised to find a female foreign exchange student as I was to find a male host student. Originally they'd planned on having their visiting student take the top bunk in Ariel's room.

That plan was scrapped the moment they met me. Instead, I've slept the last couple of nights on the couch, which is uncomfortable and lacks privacy. I wanted to go to sleep early last night—and couldn't, because Josef was up late watching BBC News. Then I was awakened by Rebecca before six in the morning, as she prepared for work.

I'm looking forward to our field trip to the Dead Sea, beginning Saturday morning. We'll be staying overnight at a hostel somewhere near Masada and I can't wait to get out of here. In the meantime, I have to deal with this. What I told Dylan was true—Ariel hasn't laid a hand on me. But his advances have been painfully obnoxious and I've never been so uncomfortable in my life.

I trudge up the stairs—that's the best I can do right now. When I enter the apartment, it's clear that Ariel said *something* to his parents, but I don't know what. At the moment he's standing in the kitchen area, back to the counter, while both of his parents speak to him in rapid, sharp words in Hebrew. I don't think they're praising his academic abilities at the moment. And when I enter the room, his eyes dart to me—then his parents' do.

Rebecca immediately turns and walks to me.

"Alexandra. Ariel tells me the two of you have had a disagreement."

With a quickly arrested laugh, I say, "You could say that. He won't leave me alone."

Josef says something in an angry tone to Rebecca. I don't know the words. She turns on him in anger and shouts something. Then she says to me, "I'm very sorry about Ariel's behavior."

Josef's eyes narrow. In his none-too-strong English, he says, "You led him on. Ariel is a good boy."

I feel instant heat on my cheeks. "I led him on?" I ask in a near rage.

"Don't listen to him," Rebecca says. "Josef is—"

She's cut off by a torrent of words in Hebrew. Not just Josef—Ariel is defending himself—at least I assume so. It's a very real handicap not knowing what anyone is saying. I turn my back on them and begin packing my bag.

That silences the room. I take the opportunity to speak. "While you all sort out who to blame, Rebecca, could you please call the exchange program? I'm afraid I can't stay here any more."

Rebecca looks almost pained. But she says what I want to hear. "Of course."

Thirty minutes later, Rebecca drives me to the hostel where our chaperones are staying. In the car, she's silent at first as she navigates through traffic. Finally, she says, "He's not a bad boy, you know. Just—things are different here." She glances at me as she says the words.

I shake my head. "I don't understand."

Her expression is one of anger. "Back home people have been concerned about sexual harassment for decades. It happens—rape happens, harassment happens—

but it's not socially approved of. Here, everything is hyper-masculine. Israel has laws against sexual harassment, but few complain. It just—it's approved of. It's covered up. Josef is wrong, but he's normal. Of course he defends Ari. Our son says he didn't *touch* you, so nothing was wrong at all."

Irrationally, I defend Ariel. "He didn't touch me."

"I know. But he wouldn't leave you alone when you asked."

"So why are you helping me now?"

She raises an eyebrow. "I'm not helping you. I can't fix my society. But I'm a mother. I can teach my son to respect women."

I blink, trying to push back unfamiliar tears. Then I whisper, "Thanks."

A moment later, after I've processed some of what she's said, I speak again. "You said, 'Back home.'"

She doesn't respond immediately. Finally she says, "I did, didn't I? Israel is my home now. But ... maybe sometimes I still think of Minneapolis that way. Everyone I know here is from somewhere else: eastern Europe, or the United States or South Africa. Josef and I are visitors. It's only *sabras* like Ariel who are *really* Israeli."

"Sabra?"

"Uh... a Jew who is born here."

"I see," I say. Hearing *facts* make me feel a little more stable. "So... you're American... why *do* you live here anyway?"

She says, "Well, that's complicated. I suppose technically I'm not American anymore—I'm an Israeli citizen. I served my three years in the military when I first moved here."

"You were in the Army?" I ask, surprised.

She nods as she scans for an opening in traffic. "Everyone serves in the army."

I nod. "What was that like?"

She shrugs. "I was in the *Mishmar Hagvul*—the, uh, border police. I spent a year in the territories near Hebron, then the rest of my enlistment in Jerusalem. That's where I met Josef."

"Did you like it?"

She shook her head. "Not really. But it was part of becoming a citizen. You sometimes have to do what you have to do. But I'm not looking forward to Ariel serving."

"Oh?"

She nods. "When I was in the territories, in the early 90s—there was hope. The Oslo Accords had been signed, and the Palestinian Authority was a new thing. I think we all held our breath for a few years. And then it all blew up in our faces in 2000 when the Arabs started killing Jews again."

I wince a little. Maybe I'm too politically correct. But I find it uncomfortable when I hear someone generalize an entire ethnic group that way. But who am I to judge? It's not like I was here to see what happened seven years ago. All I know was what I've read in books or absorbed from the news and the internet over the years. Basically, I know nothing.

For the first time in my life, I understand my dad, and have a brief moment of actually *wanting* to follow him into the Foreign Service. Imagine being in a position to help negotiate the end of a seventy-year conflict. Wouldn't the negotiators of the end of a war be responsible for saving thousands of lives? Tens of thousands? More? I told Carrie the other day that I wanted to do something meaningful with my life, after all.

But then I picture dragging my children from one country to the next. Never feeling rooted or at home. Never feeling like they were really part of something. No one talks about it, but it destroyed my parent's marriage. I've never really asked Julia what it was like when she was little, but in my entire life I've never seen my parents hold hands, or kiss each other casually, or give each other looks of affection. I always assumed that was normal, until middle school, when I would occasionally stay at friends' houses and see how *their* parents interacted with each other. I'm certain it was the stress of all the moves, and all the times my father has been away, sometimes for years at a time. I don't want that for my life. One thing I know for sure, I'll *never* get involved with a diplomat or a soldier.

Rebecca pulls the car to a stop, double parked in front of the youth hostel where we stayed the first night in Israel. She leaves her emergency lights blinking as she steps out of the car. I get out, and pull my bags out.

"I'll walk you in," she says.

I feel—awkward. And sad, really. I would have liked to have gotten to know Rebecca better. As it is, I won't have an opportunity to do so. We walk into the lobby of the hostel, where we find Marie Simpson.

Mrs. Simpson looks pensive... almost angry. As we approach, I say to Rebecca, "Thank you so much. For everything."

Rebecca gives me a sad smile. "Of course. And I'm so sorry you had to deal with that."

Awkwardly, she reaches out and hugs me. I hug back, not knowing how to feel or what to think. Rebecca backs away, leaving me with the remote and apparently angry Mrs. Simpson.

Mrs. Simpson doesn't speak until Rebecca is out of the room. Then she turns on me and says, "You couldn't wait five more days? We'll be gone two of them for the field trip anyway."

As she spits out the words, I feel myself shrink a little. I say, "What was I supposed to do? He was propositioning me constantly. Staring at me. I've never been so uncomfortable in my life."

"Which normally I would be very sympathetic to. But in your case, I'm wondering if you're just over-reacting. You've already asked for special treatment once this trip."

"I asked for *nothing*," I say. "In fact, I asked my parents to stay out of it."

She sniffs, a dismissive gesture that does nothing to calm me. "We don't have a host family for you to go to. Which means you'll be here at the hostel tonight, and probably until we leave Tel Aviv. I'm sure if I don't do that I'll be hearing about it from your father, right?"

I shrug. I don't know what to say to that. I hate how she's making me feel. Like I did something wrong. Should I have just kept quiet? After all, Ariel didn't touch me. He was just rude, and overbearing. What if I was wrong? Will he get in trouble? Will it cause trouble for me? My mother warned me to be very careful here, that everything I did would be scrutinized and exposed.

You're the child of a diplomat, Alexandra. Whether you like it or not, everything you do is public.

Sometimes I wish I was like Dylan—with parents who were invisible, at least as far as the public is concerned. From what he'd said, his family had major issues, not the least of which was his abusive father. On the other hand, he was unlikely to ever find himself on the front page of the paper because of a bad choice. My sisters and I had all learned that was a possibility the hard way. I never really learned the details—I was pretty young then, and of course no one talks about it—but years ago there was some kind of scandal involving Julia.

I try to imagine the headline: *Diplomat's daughter accuses Israeli of sexual assault.* Or worse. Reporters don't bother to find out facts, they report whatever they think will increase ratings or page views. I didn't want to be used that way.

I let out a sigh, then follow Mrs. Simpson as she leads me to what will be my new quarters. I don't know what tomorrow holds, but I'm afraid that whatever it is, it won't be good.

CHAPTER ONE

Peer Pressure!

ALEX LOOKS TIRED this morning, tense and unhappy. She has dark circles under her eyes, and as she walks toward the tour bus, she smiles less than normal. She doesn't seem to want me to approach her—since arriving at the school this morning, she's stayed close to Elle and Megan, the multi-colored-hair girl who reminds me of Spot.

Outside, the sky is grey and the air has the faintest chill of winter. Dark clouds crowd the sky, and much darker ones appear to the west. It feels like a storm coming.

I climb onto the bus and sit down next to John Modesta. John is usually pretty good about reading people, so when I close my eyes and lean my head back, he takes the hint and talks to Mike from Chicago, who sits across the aisle from us. I'm not sleepy. I just don't want to talk.

I finally set up a Facebook account night before last, as requested by Alex. After I set it up, I searched her out and added her as a friend, then promptly went looking for Spot. Unfortunately, no one using that name is on Facebook—or on MySpace, I checked that site too. If she's still alive, she's not going by her old street name.

I hate it that I don't know if she's alive or dead. I've been haunted by that. She was a good kid, and didn't deserve the crap she got. All because she liked other girls. Who the hell does that? Who rejects their children for being who they are?

I don't even have any pictures of her. It's not like I owned a fancy cell phone then (I don't now, actually). How do you look for someone when you don't have a picture of them, don't know their real name, and don't even know if they are alive?

You don't.

I looked at Alex's page last night, of course. She updates her status twenty-seven times a day. Or maybe three or four. Lots of pictures she's taken all over Tel Aviv. But this morning's status update was mysterious. It was a question.

How do you know if you're making a big deal about nothing?

I also noticed that some guy posted to her page. Michael Harrington. He said: *I haven't heard from you, babe. Miss you. Message me.*

She mentioned on the plane that she'd casually dated a guy named Mike in San Francisco. A couple of dinners and movies, nothing serious. But from the tone of his post, he seemed to think it was.

But I looked through his profile and hers, and there wasn't a single photo of the two of them together. That's a good sign. Isn't it?

I can't get my mind off Spot. It took me about twenty minutes on Facebook to find and connect with a number of friends. I didn't realize a lot of people from my school are on there, Haley included. But it's Spot I want to know about. *Is she still alive?*

Whatever. I have no way of knowing, and if I couldn't find her by searching in person for weeks, and now on-line, I probably never will. In the meantime, I've got this trip to deal with. We're headed to the Eretz Israel Museum, just on the north side of Tel Aviv. I'm not sure exactly what that's all about, but I'm hoping to find out more.

I keep my eyes closed, but start to listen in on the conversation around me. John and Mike are talking about Rami's party tonight, apparently excited about it. I've got a bad feeling. Rami was so insistent that I have a drink last night, it pissed me off. I don't drink, and I don't see any reason why anyone should try to pressure me into it. Maybe I should skip the party.

But as I glance to where Alex is sitting with Elle, I think maybe I should go after all.

Something about her.

Every time I look at Alex Thompson I feel almost overwhelmed. I've never seen a girl as beautiful as her. I've never seen a girl who arrested attention the way she does. She's not just beautiful—she's smart as hell.

She's as out of reach as if she were a princess. I'm the kid of a drunk, just a poor white trash Southern boy who got lucky enough to get nominated for this program. She's the daughter of an ambassador.

Don't get attached, Dylan. Don't let your fantasies run away with you. Because she's so far out of your league, she'll break your heart if she even looks your way.

"You all right, man?" John says the words in a low voice, not long after I opened my eyes. The bus is moving through the crowded streets of northern Tel Aviv now.

"Yeah, just tired," I say. "I didn't sleep well last night."

I glance toward the back of the bus again. Alex and Elle are having an animated conversation with Megan. Megan throws her head back and laughs and at that moment she looks so much like Spot it makes me want to cry.

In a quiet voice John asks, "What do you think of Elle?"

Uh-oh. When somebody asks a question like that, they don't want to know the truth. What I really think about Elle is that she's a giant bitch. But the words I say to John are more like, "She's great. And those legs."

He nods. "Do you think she's into me?"

I don't think she's into anyone but herself.

"Could be... I haven't seen you guys together much. What do you think?"

He shrugs. "We talked a long time the other night. And she seemed like she was leaning close to me."

"Do you like her?"

He nods. "She's beautiful."

I shrug. "If you like her, you should tell her."

He looks at me like I'm crazy. "What if she shoots me down?"

"Then... everything will be the same as it is now?"

"Huh. Good point, I guess."

My eyes land on Alex, sitting a few rows back with Elle and Megan. I give a lot of good advice to other people, don't I?

If you like her, you should tell her.

It's different with me, though. Why would a girl like her be interested in me? It's one thing to suggest to John that he talk to Elle—they're not all that different, other than the fact that John seems to be a genuinely nice guy.

At least he's not like Mike with his politics fetish. Yes, a fetish. The first day we spoke, Mike asked me my political party, and every once in a while he still needles me, trying to get an answer. Sometimes, like when he's talking about girls like any other normal teenager, he seems human. But most of the time? No.

He leans forward from the seat behind me and John and says, "Do you know, if McCain is elected, he'll be seventy-two years old when he take office? That's even older than Ronald Reagan was. And everyone knows Reagan was…"

His voice trails off into *blah blah blah*.

It's way too early in the morning for all this political talk. I nod and say *uh-huh* at what seems to be the appropriate places, but I'm not following Mike. He moves on from Ronald Reagan to a special election in Pittsburgh and how that shows that Democrats will be something or other in the coming Presidential election.

John says, "Mike, give it a rest, okay? No one cares."

By the time the bus arrives at the museum, the sky is considerably darker. My mood, too. Fat drops of rain are starting to fall from the sky. John, standing next to me as we wait to pile off the bus, says, "I didn't think it rained much here." Our chaperones, led by the grey-haired Mrs. Simpson, urge us into the museum. We crowd in, a milling mass of teenagers. John and I find ourselves jammed in directly behind Alex, Megan and Elle.

John says, "Hey, Elle." He sounds like he swallowed dry leaves before speaking.

She looks over her shoulder at him and gives him a wry smile. "You feeling okay, John?"

He coughs into his fist, then says, "Yeah. Just had something in my throat."

Alex doesn't look at me. Instead, she's on her tiptoes, trying to lean around the taller people in front of her so she can see the front of the room where Mrs. Simpson is speaking. Since John and Elle seem to be occupied, I slip in next to her and say, "Are you still mad at me?"

She drops down from her tiptoes and looks me square in the eyes. She looks calm. "No. I'm not. Still friends?"

"Yeah." *I want to be a lot more than friends.*

"Are you mad?" she asked.

"Of course not," I say. "What ended up happening, anyway?"

Mrs. Simpson says in a sharp tone, "Stop talking in the back, please."

I lower my voice, but repeat, "What ended up happening?"

She whispers, "I stayed at the youth hostel last night. Mrs. Simpson told me I'll be staying with Hadar, Elle's host student."

"Good news," I reply. Hadar is a mousy girl, short and thin, dark haired, her posture always a little slumped. She's friendly enough, but she walks around looking at the ground all the time. She needs to get some confidence. Ironically, her best friend is Levona, Megan's host student. Levona is one of the loudest girls I've ever known. They make a funny pair.

Mrs. Simpson shoots me a dirty look. I stop talking. A man is now addressing the students. He's tall, and like everyone in Israel, he is casually dressed, wearing blue jeans and a green golf shirt. It's an awful green, really, not quite lime-colored. He begins to speak, introducing himself as the director of the museum.

For the next three hours we move in the group throughout the several buildings of the museum looking at archeological finds: jewelry and pottery, weapons and coins. The museum sits on the site of a 12th Century BCE archaeological mound, an ancient Philistine city. It's interesting stuff, and as I walk through, I find myself wondering if I should start thinking more seriously about college. Alex was shocked the other day when I told her I hadn't picked any schools to apply to. It's November of my senior year in high school.

What *am* I going to do next year?

Unlike most of the kids I'm walking through the museum with, I don't have the kind of grades that will get me into an Ivy League college. My SAT scores were very high, but I'll be lucky to graduate in the top half of my class. That said, Georgia State is still in option. I'd also considered a couple of other state universities— SUNY Stony Brook, for instance, has a good creative writing program. But then I get stuck on wondering how I would possibly pay for college. It's not like my Mom is rolling in money. I can't ask her to take on student loans for me. It's been nearly three years since she got sober, and she's still pulling her life together. Saddling her with fifty thousand dollars in debt is just not an option. I can take my own student loans, but the math doesn't work out. And with my pathetic 2.4 grade point average, I won't be getting any scholarships.

Which still leaves the option of the Army. I've talked to the recruiters more than once. They come around to the high school every couple of months. I get emails from the Army almost every week. Postcards too, though my mother throws those in the trash. I've spoken with her once about the Army—she was opposed to the idea.

There's a war going on, Dylan. A stupid war, a pointless stupid war that is destroying people's lives for nothing.

I don't know what to say to that. Of course I know there's a war on—it's been going on since I was ten years old. But the existence of the war shouldn't keep me from going into the military. In fact, it should be the opposite. Sometimes I feel like I need to join the Army *because* we're at war. I mean, if no one enlists, if no one goes voluntarily, then how does our country defend itself?

I may not be into politics like John is, but I do love my country. I'm not afraid to go to war. And it *would* pay for me to go to college.

By lunchtime, it has long since stopped raining. Our group moves outside to a covered outdoor dining area with picnic tables. I end up bunched at one table with Mike from Chicago, John, Alex, Elle and Megan. As soon as we sit down, Mike says, "Who's going to Rami's party tonight?"

John and Elle both say, simultaneously, "I'll be there." Then they burst into laughter. Megan nods. "I'm going. You?"

"Yeah, I'll be there," Mike says. He slaps me on the shoulder. "What about you, Dylan?"

I swallow. If I've judged Dari correctly, the party is going to involve a lot of alcohol. "I don't know," I say.

Elle turns to Alex. "Well, *you* have to come, Alex. I already talked with Hadar, she's planning on going, and you can't just stay at home alone."

Alex's eyes meet mine, then jerk away. Then she smiles, a second too late, and says, "I'll be there."

"Come on, Dylan!" John yells. "Peer pressure! Peer pressure!"

I laugh. "Fine. But just know, I don't drink, and if Rami keeps pushing me on it, I'll end up popping him in the nose."

Mike says, "I believe it, after yesterday."

I cough. Mike has the bad grace to keep going. "I can't *believe* you went after Ariel like that. Dude is *huge*."

"He's a huge asshole," Alex says. The rest of them burst into laughter, and I smile. Her comment cuts the tension.

Mike says, in a loud mock Israeli accent, "Get out of way if you want to live." Then he claps me on the shoulder. I try to restrain my annoyance.

And if so... if ... I mean (Alex)

"Damn it, I can't find my lipstick!" As Elle half shouts, half whines the words, she bounces a little on her feet. In the last ten minutes, she's torn her suitcase open and strewn her clothing and God only knows what other possessions over half the room. Elle is wearing insufficient clothing for November, and has carefully drawn cat-eyes under her expertly-curled bangs.

Hadar looks almost startled when she enters the room and sees Elle. The poor girl is so self-effacing, it's a wonder she speaks at all. She gives Elle a timid smile and says, "My mother has some lipstick... maybe you could use some?" Her statement confirms that Elle's outburst was loud—Hadar was in the living room watching reruns of Grey's Anatomy at too high a volume.

Elle sighs. Then says, "May I?" in a sickly sweet fake voice.

I really don't like her much at all. She follows Hadar out of the room—undoubtedly to raid Hadar's mother's makeup stash.

I sigh, relieved they've left the room. Everything else aside, I was incredibly grateful to sleep in a room by myself last night. Except for summer camps and the occasional sleepover (always at someone else's house),

I've never had to share a room before. I feel crowded and stressed, and appreciate these few seconds to myself. I take out my phone—Julia bought me an iPhone the day it was first released last summer. It's an expensive indulgence, and a nice toy, but it's also been essential since I got to Israel.

I pull up Facebook on my phone—my data connection has been awful since I arrived here, but Hadar's family has wifi.

Mike has posted on my wall, again. *I miss you, Alexandra xo xo xo*. He's starting to get annoying. We only went out a few times.. He put more xo's in his wall post than we've had dates. I seriously need to talk to him.

Out of curiosity, I visit Dylan's page, which he just set up. He doesn't appear to have updated it at all—no photo, no posts, though it says he's friended several people. I look at their pages. Most of them seem to be from his high school.

I frown when I see *Hayley Briggs*. That's the girl he said he's been out with a few times. *It's not serious*, he told me. Without really paying attention, I find myself looking through her photos. She takes what appears to be 250 selfies every day. Duck lips. Lots of them. She looks—vacuous. Overly made-up. Nowhere in any of her pictures, or anywhere on her wall, is there mention of or any sign of a book. Maybe she's never read one. Plenty of mentions of Justin Timberlake, Britney Spears, Kanye West, Alicia Keys. She posts her opinion almost daily of *Keeping Up With the Kardashians*.

What could this girl possibly have to interest a serious, smart guy like Dylan?

Oh—I know. Blonde hair, tiny waist and big boobs.

I hate her. She posted on Dylan's wall the day after he created his Facebook account: *Missed me that much? When you get home, I've got something really hot for you.*

Slut.

I smile grimly when I realize he didn't even bother to click *Like* on her post.

Oh no. No. No. I *can't* get this hung up on a guy. Especially not a guy who lives thousands of miles from me. This trip is only for a few weeks. Have I lost my mind?

I put away my phone. I hate everything. The door opens and Elle and Hadar re-enter the room. Both of them are wearing garish red lipstick. Elle sees something in my face—she immediately says, "What's wrong?"

"Nothing," I say. I stare at the wall as I say it.

"Nothing?"

"Nothing."

"I don't believe you," she replies.

I swallow. Then I say, "Do you think Dylan likes me? Like really?"

Elle says in a sarcastic tone, "Ya think?"

I feel my eyebrows scrunch together. "What is that supposed to mean?"

"Girl, he's got it bad for you. Puppy love. His eyes follow you everywhere. How have you not noticed?"

"There's a girl he's gone out with back home. Look," I blurt out. I unlock my phone and show her the photo of Skanky Hayley.

"Nice phone," Elle says.

I immediately pout, and she looks at the picture. She raises an eyebrow. "Well, I bet *she's* not a virgin."

Hadar blushes three shades of red. I want to sink into the floor. Elle sits on the bed next to me. "Alex—Dylan is a different kind of guy. I mean—he's real. Like *really* real."

What the hell does that mean? She keeps going. "I don't think he'd fall for that for long. He's a smart guy. You should tell him you like him."

I shake my head violently.

Elle smiles and leans close. "Get some confidence, girl. Confidence is attractive. And he seriously likes you already. Blow him a kiss or something and he'll come running. I guarantee it."

I'm nervous. So nervous. Because he agreed to be at the party at Rami's tonight, and I'm going to be there, and I hardly know what to say to him. I hardly know what to do or to think.

What if he hates me?

We have dinner with Hadar's parents at seven, and it seems like it takes four hours. In fact, we eat in an intense silence, finishing in just a few minutes. Then we sit there fidgeting while the rest of the family eats. Hadar's father Samuel stares at his plate. Her mother and sister chatter away about some Israeli television show, then move on from that to who knows what. I don't, because they unconsciously shifted into Hebrew, which makes sense really since the rest of us aren't talking. Eventually even the Hebrew conversation drops off.

It's almost as tense as dinner at home.

After a few minutes, Samuel sighs. Then he says at a near shout, "All right. Go!"

Hadar jumps to her feet, then gives her Dad a kiss on the cheek. "I love you, Daddy." Then she runs out of the room.

Elle and I follow. As we're getting light jackets on, Hadar kisses her father on the cheek. Then we're out on the street, walking the five blocks to Rami's apartment.

The air outside is crisp, though not quite cold yet. I can't really tell if the sky is clear: Ramat Gan has a dense skyline, including some of the tallest skyscrapers in this part of the world, so even on a good night the stars are nearly invisible.

This neighborhood, a mile or so south of the Diamond Exchange, features a series of blocky-looking apartment buildings, each about three stories high and standing on narrow stilts, with parking below the buildings. I've never liked houses on stilts, though you see them often enough in San Francisco. It seems crazy to me. Every few months we have minor earthquakes, and every few years we have major ones. Why would anyone put their house on top of a bunch of toothpicks?

Rami's building is more or less indistinguishable from Hadar's. We follow her under the building, then inside and up the stairs. It's easy to tell which apartment is Rami's—I can hear music coming from the apartment as we reach the top of the stairs. I recognize the song—*Push the Button* by Teapacks. The song is wildly popular in Israel. The exhortations of the singer to *Push the Button* gives a window into just how jaded and cynical young people here are. I've seen a lot of it in the last few days. Everyone here needs a dose of anxiety medication.

Of course, if you live with the periodic threat of rocket attacks and suicide bombers, you'd need meds, too.

Rami's door is propped open with a chair, and the tiny apartment, laid out almost exactly like Hadar's, is crowded with teenagers. As we enter, Rami shouts, "Hello! Hadar! Alex! *Elle!!!*" He calls Elle's name in a growling, mock-masculine way. He might as well shout *please fuck me.* Elle purses her lip and ignores him. Hadar blushes. I just keep moving, into the apartment and past Rami. Hadar, who seems to have shrunk three sizes, stays close behind me.

Elle, on the other hand, immediately starts talking with Kobi, one of the guys from the high school. I think Mike is staying with him. Kobi is a big guy, muscular, one of those overly masculine bodybuilders who might look pretty from a distance but probably has little more than a couple of marbles rolling around in his head. That's about her speed—I have the feeling Elle's going to want to dominate any guy she ever comes into contact with.

Beyond the small foyer and entryway is a rectangular living room and a small balcony. I look around, disoriented at first, overwhelmed by the large number of teenagers jammed into the small space. Then I spot Dylan Paris.

He's in one corner of the room. A can of Coke, letters in Hebrew, sits open in front of him, and a burning cigarette dangles from his mouth. He has his eyes closed, head leaning back, his right hand strumming his guitar, his left hand fingering the chords. He doesn't look at the instrument as he plays, and he doesn't notice me as he pops the cigarette out of his mouth and drops it in the Coke can, then begins to sing. *House of the Rising Sun.* I only know the song because Julia is such a snob about music, there's always something unusual playing whenever she's visiting.

His singing voice is untrained, a little artless, but sincere in a way I think Julia would appreciate. Rough around the edges, a little gravelly. I catch my breath as he launches into the song. I'm not the only one. Hadar, standing next to me, stops talking and stares openly. Megan, her hair unusually erect and colorful this evening, can't take her eyes off of him. I want to punch them both.

But then he opens his eyes and looks directly at me. He nods, just slightly, as if to acknowledge my presence, and continues playing. He ignores everyone else in the room.

I'm in an intense state of anxiety, fear and anticipation. My stomach is tied up, my heart is beating fast, the skin on my face is hot. I step out of the room and head to the kitchen, then get myself a drink of water. I need to get a hold of myself.

I stand at the sink, gulping the water down. I close my eyes as I set the glass down, taking a long, calming breath. Okay. I can do this. I'm being ridiculous. I open my eyes and turn around, intending to head back into the living room, and bump directly into Dylan Paris.

Give me some credit. I don't squeak or squeal or anything else my mother would call unladylike. But I am *very* startled. By the looks of it, so is he, because he takes a sudden step back.

"Dylan?"

"Hey," he says. "Um…"

"Uh…." I say, adding to the awkwardness.

"Listen, do you have a minute?" he asks.

Do I have a minute? For what? Is he going to tell me he doesn't want me around? To leave him alone?

Alex: *Get. A. Grip.*

I cough. "Yes," I say. My voice cracks a little. He says, "Can we talk in private?" His eyes dart to the other people in the room. I nod, and he leads me toward the back of the apartment, and we slip into a bedroom. I assume it's Rami's, for no adult would have a room with posters of rock stars, among… other things.

Dylan gestures to the bed. I stop, startled, then blush horribly. He couldn't have meant—

"Oh…" he says. "I mean… sit down?" He says it like a question, and he sits, too suddenly. His eyes are looking everywhere but me. Like he's nervous.

I sit down too. Next to him, but slightly away, so I'm turned slightly toward him. And I wait.

And wait.

He swallows, looks at me, then looks away.

What? Is there something on my face?

I almost reach for my face to see, when he blurts out, "I was telling John earlier that if he likes Elle, he should just tell her, you know? Because, if he never tells her, it's definitely a no, right? And if he does, the worst that can happen is she says no, so why not?"

I blink, feeling a sinking, sad feeling. I'd hoped... I'd *really* hoped... that Dylan was... you know. Asking me out. And ... instead he's talking about John. Probably wants to know whether or not Elle likes John. I start to say, "I don't really know if she—"

He interrupts. "No. I'm not asking about her."

I shake my head slowly. "I don't understand."

"It's just, since I'm giving out advice to people, I guess I should follow it, right? But the thing is, we're only here for a few weeks. And then that's it. We go back to the United States, and I live in Atlanta and you live in California and..."

As he talks, I feel heat rising to my face. Is he... wait... he's not asking about John and Elle...

"Anyway, the thing is, Alex, I'm... really attracted to you. A lot." As he says the words, his blue eyes keep me pinned to my seat.

He sits there, waiting for me to respond. And I'm struggling to know what to say. So he continues. "Anyway, I guess I was wondering if you felt the same way. And if so... if ... I mean... I ... we..."

He starts drowning in a pool of inarticulateness, so I throw him a lifeline. "I do."

"You do?"

I nod.

He smiles. "We're only here for a few weeks."

I reply. "It couldn't be anything permanent."

He shrugs. "Right. But for now..."

"We can..."

He nods.
I do too.

CHAPTER SEVEN

Why wasn't I invited? (Dylan)

I T'S QUIET—ALMOST 2:30 am. Dari, across the room from me, is snoring lightly. It's not loud. Just loud enough to keep me awake, tossing and turning.

Except, let's be honest. It isn't Dari's snoring that's keeping me awake. It's the party at Rami's.

My mind pores over the evening. I stayed in the corner for the first hour, just smoking and playing my guitar. Sticking to myself, because *everyone* was drinking, and I don't drink, and I'll never drink, because for me drinking is death. Or close enough to death you can hardly tell the difference. One look at Lawrence Paris is enough. One thought of him, one thought of his sarcasm, his bitterness, his abusive words and fists, is enough to remind me that I don't ever want to be him. I don't want to be anything *like* him.

I don't know what I was thinking asking Alex out.

Anyway, the thing is, Alex, I'm... really attracted to you. A lot.

I'm laying on my back, staring at the ceiling. Asking myself over and over again, did I make a mistake? That moment when she answered. Her eyes widened a little as I spoke, her pupils dilated, slight color on her cheeks. Her lips separated just enough to let a breath out before she whispered the words "I do."

I close my eyes, feeling the warmth of those words. The warmth of her eyes. We stayed and talked for a long time, before she finally left with Elle and Hadar. After, I walked the three blocks back to Dari's apartment in a daze. He asked me what was wrong on the way back. My answer: "Nothing. Nothing at all."

He must have thought I was crazy.

I do.

This can never last. We're only here for a few weeks, and that's probably a good thing, because I would screw it up for sure. I'm not cut out to be her boyfriend. She's an ambassador's daughter. I'm a ... a nobody.

I sigh, thinking of how the light played over her hair. We hadn't kissed. We just talked. For a long time. On her way out of the apartment, she put a hand on my shoulder and whispered in my ear, "I like you, Dylan Paris."

Those words made me feel like I'd had a few drinks. I won't lie. Lightheaded. Dazed. I can still smell the faint strawberry smell of her hair.

I turn over on my right side, pulling the blanket over my head.

Then I sigh. I'm wide awake. I sneak a peek out from under the blanket to the clock on the table beside Dari's bed.

2:45. I've been laying here almost two hours.

I sit up. I'm wasting my time trying to sleep right now. Instead, I slip out of the bed, trying to be quiet. I don't want to wake Dari up. I tiptoe toward the door. He doesn't stir. I slide the pocket door open, step into the hall and slide it closed.

In the living room is an old iMac. It's on, the screensaver showing a succession of images of Dari, his parents and siblings on their various trips around Israel and Europe. The screensaver vanishes when I move the mouse. I check first to make sure the volume is off, then open a browser.

I don't know where Spot is, but I *do* know the names of a few people who knew her. Scott McLellan knew her—I went to school with him freshman year, before both of us dropped out and went our separate ways. I'd returned to school. He ended up in rehab. It wasn't likely, but it was *possible* he had an account.

Bingo.

Scott McLellan of Atlanta, Georgia. 19 years old. I didn't realize he was older than me. In his profile picture, he looks a lot older than last time I saw him. He had a scraggly beard covering his pockmarked face in uneven patches.

My mouse hovers over the "Add Friend" for too long. I finally click on it.

I take a breath. I didn't realize I'd been holding my breath. But I had. I close my eyes for a second and give myself a pep talk. Something like, *Dude, get it together*. Then I take another long breath and click on the message button. Quickly I type in a message:

Scott! How's it going? I know we were never good friends, but we knew some of the same people. I've been looking for Spot. You ever hear anything about her? Take it easy. Dylan.

I almost gasp as I finish typing the message. Scott represents some of the worst of my past. I remember sitting around in the alley behind the Masquerade, passing around a joint and sometimes a bottle. Scott was a major asshole sometimes—he would jerk people around. Take their money, make promises he couldn't keep. For a while there he let Spot think he might have a place she could go to stay long term. He was angling to get her to sleep with him, no matter that she wasn't into guys. What she wanted wouldn't have mattered to a guy like Scott anyway.

But if he knows where she is, I want to talk to him.

I go back to Alex's page. Then I freeze.

Her status is two words: I do.

That's followed by a barrage of comments from friends, the first one from a Carrie Thompson. That must be one of her sisters. Carrie wrote, **You do? To who? When? Why wasn't I invited?**

I click on to Carrie's page. Her profile picture is a shock. Beautiful woman, kneeling as a *mountain lion* licks her face. That's one ballsy chick. Who does that? She's beautiful, but not like Alex. Alex is like the sun, Carrie a pale (very pale) shadow beside her.

I sigh. It's 3:30, and I'm still not sleepy. Figures. I'll crash right about when it's time to get up. I look up a couple more people who might know Spot. I don't want to reestablish contact with any of these people. They represent a life that isn't mine anymore, a life I don't need or want to have any part of.

I sigh and close my eyes. Funny, I never even thought to look online for her. Until Alex suggested it, I'd never been on Facebook, I didn't see the point. Same with MySpace. Bunch of people taking selfies and making weird faces at themselves in mirrors. But once I'd gotten on here, and people I knew from school started popping up—now I was obsessed. Because *somebody* must know what happened to her.

Enough. It's time for bed. I log out of Facebook, step away from the computer, and quietly slip back to the bed.

Sleepy? (Alex)

It's six forty-five in the morning in Ramat Gan as I stumble behind Elle along the sidewalk toward the tour bus. At six forty-five here, it's … what… eight-forty five at night in California? I think so. I've lost track. I've lost track of where I am and what day it is, partly because on top of the jet-lag, which is *finally* hitting me, I was up late.

Really late.

No sooner had we gotten to the street last night when Elle jumped up and down and squealed. Understand—Elle is from New York and normally talks in a sort of sultry, Sophia Loren voice. To be honest, I think she practices it when she's alone, because it certainly doesn't sound natural. But the squeal? That is natural. And grating.

"He asked me out!" she shouted.

"He?" I knew that Dylan had given John a pep-talk about asking out Elle, so I knew the answer to my own question. I asked because Elle annoyed me. She was so self-centered, I could probably have made out with Dylan right in front of everybody and she wouldn't have noticed. So we walked back to Hadar's house (Hadar trailing behind us, as if she were the guest and not the other way around), with Elle talking a thousand words a minute about John Modesta. He's *so* cute and *so* smart and *so* masculine. She didn't say that he was gruff, opinionated, and sometimes uncivil—also characteristics of his. Though to be fair, John and Dylan seemed to be getting to be pretty good friends.

Whatever. What *did* happen was that Elle talked about John to the exclusion of anything (or anybody) else until nearly two in the morning. By the end of it, Hadar and I both had glassy eyes and I was almost regretting leaving Ariel AKA hormone-boy's house. His carnal advances were actually easier to fend off than Elle's voice.

Eventually, though, Hadar noted, "I saw you and Dylan talking a long talk."

"A long *time*," Elle said. Like I said. Annoying.

"Yeah. "I found myself biting my lip as I looked at Hadar. "He um… asked me out."

At that, Hadar squealed, probably the loudest sound I'd ever heard from her.

My point is, it was three in the morning before I finally got to sleep. Then up again not quite three hours later. I'm bleary-eyed as I stumble toward the tour bus, a long, monster-sized bus with a large cargo area underneath. I join the line of students loading their stuff, and throw my bag in.

The bus driver, a youngish Israeli man in an olive-green t-shirt, his face looking as if he shaved it no more than once a week, poked at the cargo area, repositioning bags. Once mine was in place, I turn away and come face to face with Dylan.

He gives me a crooked smile. "Morning," he says. He's tired—I can tell, because his southern accent, often barely detectable, is now pretty thick.

"Good morning to you," I say. I feel heat on my cheeks. He leans in and tosses his bag into the cargo area under the bus, then slips his hand around my forearm.

"Sit with me?" he asks.

I open my mouth to say something, but I literally *can't*. No one is this confident. He must be faking it. Or he's drunk. Or—I don't know. But the touch of his fingertips along the inside of my arm sends a flare of lightning right up my nerve pathways. So I just follow him. He stops next to one of the pairs of seats. Typical tour bus fare, much like we've seen already on this trip—comfortable, multicolored seats of fabric with thick padding and comfortable arms. This bus has electric plugs at each row, which *isn't* all that common.

"After you," he says.

I feel a shiver run straight up my back. I slip into the window seat, and he slides in beside me.

"You'll have to forgive me," he says, his voice still sounded more slurred than usual. "I didn't sleep well last night, I'm pretty out of it."

"I didn't either," I say. "Elle had me up talking half the night."

"Oh yeah?" he says, raising one eyebrow. "What about?"

"Like I'd tell you," I say. My words are a little harsh, but my tone isn't. I elaborate: "Girl talk."

His eyes move to the sidewalk outside the bus. John and Elle are standing together. He has an arm casually wrapped around her, one hand *almost* touching her butt. Dylan says, "I'm guessing it had something to do with John boy there."

I sigh and roll my eyes. He just chuckles. A few minutes later, Mrs. Simpson stands at the front of the bus and counts off the group, just in case we left someone behind. Everyone's aboard. None of the Israeli host students are along for this trip, which I'll admit is a bit of a relief. I like Hadar, but the group as a whole can be very overwhelming. As Mrs. Simpson finishes checking everyone, the bus driver says something to her—I don't quite catch the words—and then he puts the bus in gear and we pull out into traffic. The bus heads toward Bar Illon University—only a few blocks from the high school—then south on Highway 4. It's slow going getting out of the city—commuter traffic in and out of Tel Aviv is extremely heavy.

"Tell me something," Dylan says. *Something* comes out almost like *sum-thin*.

I lean against the window and look at him. His eyes are a little red—he's genuinely exhausted. In this state, his lips naturally curl up just a little, a sort of crooked smile that is far sexier than is healthy.

Shiver. I feel a wave of lightweight emotion. I just want to reach out and touch him.

Tentatively... very tentatively... I do. I let my hand slide toward his, just barely. I don't actually take his hand. I just let mine rest next to his, our skin just touching.

He takes my hand in his. I close my eyes and breathe deeply.

"Tell you what?" I ask. The words feel unnatural, because it feels like 95 percent of my attention is fixated on our hands, fingers casually intertwined. As if we did this every day. As if it wasn't earth shattering on some level.

He shrugs. "Something. What is your life like?"

I feel lightheaded as I speak. "It's pretty normal, I guess. I go to school. Piano lessons. Study. I've got friends."

"Do you have a best friend?"

I nod. "Renee. My dad retired and we moved back to San Francisco when I was starting middle school. Everybody knew everyone else—except me. I was the strange kid who had lived in China and Russia but hardly ever in America. Renee was the other new girl. The first day of school no one talked to me or her, so we ended up next to each other by default."

"Where is she from?"

"Renee's from Alaska."

Surprise registers on his face. "Really? How did she end up in San Francisco?"

I'm still trying to keep my attention on him and his questions—not our hands, which are still intertwined. It's hard to focus. "Her dad works works for some internet company. I don't know what he does. But she lives just a couple of blocks from me. Which is good, because sometimes I just need to get away, you know?"

He tilts his head. "Like, from home?"

I nod. "I love my sisters... and my parents and all... but they're not like other people."

"How so?"

I shrug. "I don't know how to explain it. Dad's—remote. He stays wrapped up in his work. He's always worried, always thinking about important things. People's lives depend on him, you know?"

"What about your mom?"

I don't want to answer that question. I give Dylan a somewhat bitter smile and just shake my head. He looks puzzled, so I say in a very quiet voice, "My mom's kind of unstable."

He nods and squeezes my hand—not hard, just reassuring. "I get it. My mom—she's pretty squared away now, but back in the day she was one sandwich short of a picnic. Always liquored up. Dad too. Maybe not the same kind of crazy as yours, but crazy."

I take a deep breath and squeeze his hand back. Then I find myself, in horror, yawning.

"Sleepy?" he asks, his smile quirking up.

"Yeah," I say.

"Me too. Why don't you lay on my shoulder?"

Oh. My. God.

Yes, he just said that. I think he even meant it. I do, pulling my legs up close so I can turn in my seat and rest my head on his shoulder. He slumps down a little and leans his head against mine.

Will I even be able to sleep like this? I'm so aware of his skin against mine. He has a little stubble on his chin, and I can just make out the slight tobacco smell in his hair—not stinky, because it's very faint.

His breathing slows, and mine does . I can't shut off my stupid brain. It circles and circles. We're only together for a few weeks. Then it's back to our normal lives. And the thought of going home, of saying good-bye, already scares me.

I slowly drift off to sleep. And find myself dreaming.

Dylan is in San Francisco, the two of us walking along Golden Gate Park. It's a fanciful day, the sky blue, flowers blooming in a riot of colors. A confusing crowd of people surrounds us—crowds in China, a paper dragon, a group of frowning, dour diplomats lined up in a row. But Dylan is smiling and laughing.

In the way of dreams, however, we don't stay there. Instead, we're standing in front of my parents, who stare at me and Dylan in disapproval. Dad is talking, and his words are harsh, but I don't understand him. But it's clear enough what he means. Because Dylan lets go of my hand and turns away. Dad folds his arms across his chest, a self-satisfied look on his face. Mom turns her back on him.

I jerk awake, my heart pounding.

Oh, God, that was awful.

I'm still leaning on Dylan's shoulder, his head against mine. Our hands aren't touching. He's breathing deeply—far gone in slumber. I shift positions a little and close my eyes again.

I reach out and put my hand on his.

Chapter Eight

That was awkward (Dylan)

DRAMA.

It started in the late afternoon, not long before we arrived at the Ein Gedi Guest House after a long journey. Through the course of the day, we'd visited an air base in Be'ersheva, including the museum there which depicted Israel's many wars with its neighbors. From there, we'd gone to an art gallery after lunch, then gotten on the bus again for the ride here.

Ein Gedi is an oasis not far from the Dead Sea (where we will be going tomorrow) and the Qumran caves, where the Dead Sea scrolls were found. The hostel is almost luxurious, but right now things are tense as John and I get ready to head to dinner.

That's because, after all of 12 hours of dating, Elle and John broke up.

I don't know what it was about. All I know is that as Alex and I were huddled together in our seats on the tour bus about an hour into the drive, Elle suddenly appeared at my shoulder.

"Excuse me. Alex, can I talk with you?" Elle's eyes were filled with tears.

Christ on a crutch, what now?

Of course, Alex went with Elle, leaving me sitting alone. After the long day sitting together, walking together in the museums and at the air base, I felt bereft.

Unfortunately, moment's later John filled that spot.

"Kids, stay in your seats," Mrs. Simpson said. "No more moving around."

Great.

"What's wrong?" I asked.

"Elle dumped me."

"You guys haven't been together long enough for her to dump you."

"No, really." He looked distraught.

"Why?" I asked.

"I don't know!"

And that was about as much as I learned during the final thirty minutes of the drive. I was thanking God when we arrived at the hostel. At least I could get something to eat soon, and grab a cigarette.

It hasn't gotten any better in the half hour since. John seems despondent, and he has no clue what is going on. I'm no closer to getting a smoke than I was an hour ago. Finally I say, "Hey, I'm going outside before dinner, all right? You can join me if you still want to talk."

Of course he does. He follows me down the hall, to the stairs, then out front. I want nothing more than to be left alone right now. Well, that's not true. I want to see Alex right now. But if I can't do that, then let me have some blessed solitude. That's been the one downside of this trip—I just don't get enough time alone.

That doesn't look like it's going to change anytime soon. I find my way out of the hostel to a balcony overlooking the valley and the Dead Sea below. It's a re-markable sight. Just on the other side of the prome-nade, and stretching all the way to the Dead Sea and the mountains beyond, is a barren brown landscape. In the distance, the mountains of Jordan tower over the Dead Sea, fading into deep reds and purples. The sun will be setting soon.

The oasis, surrounding the guest house, is *green*. Lush trees and bushes, palm and olive trees, thick grass.

I cup a flame in my hand, lighting my cigarette, then take a deep drag. The smoke going down my throat is calming, and I close my eyes and just soak in the environment. The air is warm, and the smells from the lush plantlife of the oasis are sweet, almost floral.

This would be a good place to meditate.

Well, it would be if I didn't have John standing be-side me.

"I just don't understand *why*," he says.

"Maybe you should ask her."

"Ask her? What am I supposed to say?"

I sigh. And open my mouth. Then close it, because nothing I would say right now would be constructive. What goes through my head is that Elle is a giant bitch, and she's probably just playing with him. Normally I'm not this judgmental of people—no, seriously. But in this case, I'm pretty sure I'm right. Yesterday she was all over him like a cheap suit, and now she's dumped him? She's playing some kind of game with him, and it isn't very nice.

"I don't know, man," I finally say. "I don't know Elle that well, but it seems to me, if you guys can't stay together for more than twelve hours...."

"Don't say it," he replies.

I shrug and take a last drag of my smoke. The cigarette, a Palestinian brand called Farid, has a noticeably sweet, pungent smell, nothing like American cigarettes—but also much cheaper. I stamp it out under my foot, then toss the filter in a trash can and head back inside, trusting that John will follow.

He does. A few minutes later we walk into the large dining hall in the hostel. The students from our group take up four large round tables. Each table has plain brightly colored plates in front of each place, and several large dishes in the center. Hummus, meats of various kinds, breads, desserts.

Alex and Elle are sitting at the same table, with two empty spaces beside them, which may prove to be awkward. I don't consult with John about this—instead, I walk directly toward Alex and slip into the seat beside her.

"Hey," I say.

She immediately brightens, her teeth showing white, and that makes me want to touch her lips. We haven't kissed.

I don't know when or if we will.

But I want to.

Then John sits down in the seat next to Elle, who looks decidedly ornery. Neither of them speaks. In fact, none of the others at the table say a word. Instead, they all watch the unfolding drama that is John and Elle.

I'm not getting into that. Instead, I reach forward and pull a half sandwich to my plate along with some pita bread, then take a large helping of hummus. There are several pitchers on the table, including a carafe of what looks like coffee. Score. I pour myself a cup of coffee, mix in too much sugar and milk, and get started eating.

"Baby," John whispers, as if the rest of the kids at the table weren't straining their ears trying to listen in.

"Shut up," Elle responds.

"So," Megan says. "What did you guys think of the art museum?"

Well, that's awkward.

Mike adds to the awkwardness by saying, "That place was … something." It was that. Something. The museum, housed in an Ottoman style former governor's mansion, was in fact pretty interesting. But right now, no one could remember any of the exhibits.

"Baby," John pleads.

I swear Elle's face turns red and her eyes turn up in the corners. "You should tell all of them what you did."

Mike says, in a conversational tone, "I don't know that's really necessary—"

"All right!" John says. He turns toward the rest of us, and says in a whining, too loud tone, "I tried to grab her boob! All right? Is that so bad?"

The entire room goes silent. Including our chaperones, led by Mrs. Simpson, who sits in the corner, her eyes now fixed on John.

"Smooth," Elle says. "Real smooth."

I shake my head. Alex looks at me, and appears to be biting her lip in an effort to keep from laughing. I lean toward her and say, "What do you say we finish eating and blow this joint? Go take a walk."

She nods. She's still biting her lip, but her expression is different. A little excited.

It already is (Alex)

When Dylan and I walk out of the hostel to the promenade, it's dark. The sky is clear, and I can see more stars than are ever visible in San Francisco. Dylan walks along beside me, holding my hand, staring up at the sky.

"Look at that," he says. "That's heaven, right there in front of us." He points at the sky. "There's the Big Dipper. And the Little Dipper. And Orion."

I shake my head. "I don't know anything about stars."

He smiles, then pulls me close to him, putting an arm around my waist. He stands close behind me and points so I can follow the line of his arm.

"See... the Big Dipper's right there. You can see the handle, and the cup. Right?"

I do sort of see it. Seven stars, looking all the world like a sauce pan with a bent handle. "Why don't they call it the Big Sauce Pan?"

He says, "Don't ask snarky questions. Now, look here... if you follow those two stars at the end of the Big Dipper..."

"Where?" I ask. The cool air is blowing at me, but I don't feel it. All I feel is the warmth of his arm around my waist.

"Follow it right along the line of those two stars. Right... over ... here... do you see the Little Dipper? And right there on the end is the North Star."

"Really?" It looks faint, just a pattern of stars, the one of the end—the North Star—not even closest to the brightest of the bunch. "I always assumed the North Star would be brighter, or something."

"Nah," he says. "Nothing special about it like that. It's just that it's lined up with the north pole, so if you can find the Big Dipper... and from that the Little Dipper and the North Star... you can always find your way, because you always know which way is north."

I shiver a little. "Did you take an astronomy class or something?"

"My Dad taught me. Back when I was little. Before he got too mean. I was a Cub Scout for a little while."

"Really?" I ask.

He nods. "Yeah. But ... then I couldn't stay in. I don't know what happened. Dad got in a fight with somebody about something on the first camping trip we went on. I'd guess he was drinking, and someone said something to him. We didn't go back after that."

I find myself picturing Dylan as a little boy. Blue uniform, with his father on a camping trip. Then not being able to stay in the scouts, and not knowing why.

"You must have been sad," I say.

In a guarded tone, he says, "I don't know. I tried not to have too many expectations."

We sit down on the stone wall along the edge of the promenade. Far below, we can see the road along the edge of the Dead Sea, a tiny pair of headlights, all alone, moving from south to north.

"What about now?" I ask. "Do you have expectations now?"

He shrugs. "You start expecting too much, you set yourself up for disappointment."

I find myself intertwining my fingers with his. I whisper, "You know... we don't have to worry about that. About disappointment. I mean... we don't have much time anyway."

He nods. "Yeah. It's true."

Then he leans forward and kisses me.

It happens so suddenly I didn't expect it. Or plan on it. I've never kissed a boy before. But he is confident, his lips pressing against mine, everything suddenly washed in a warm glow, but I'm also incredibly self-conscious. What if I'm doing this wrong? Will he think I don't know what I'm doing? He's been with girls before. He's eighteen. But what if I *am* good at it? Will he think I've kissed boys before? Will he think I'm easy? I find myself shaking a little, shivering with sensation as he puts his left hand on my waist. His right hand runs along the base of my jaw, fingertips just barely touching my skin.

It's a full minute before we come up for air. Then we're staring in each other's eyes. Even in this dim light, I can see the striking blue.

"This could get complicated," I say.

He just grins. "It already is." Then he leans forward and kisses me again.

Chapter Nine

Must not hate (Dylan)

WHEN I SIT down at the table, I'm seated to the right of Yossi's great-grandmother, a sour-faced woman who seems to spend most of her days sitting on the balcony overlooking the national park, slowly knitting with knobby hands.

To her left is Yossi's mother, Dana. She's not quite forty, and looks young for her age, but has worry-lines on her face. Yossi, my host student, is a seventeen-year-old high school senior. His younger brother Ramzy sits to my right.

I haven't met the boys' father or heard any mention of him. I'm a little sensitive myself about absent fathers, so I haven't asked. But I'm intensely curious. The only reference I've seen is an 8x10 black and white photograph in the living room, showing a man in the green uniform of an Israeli reservist. In the photo, he looks like he is in his thirties, and he has a broad smile on his face. Yossi casually said, "My father," when he was showing me around the house. But that's all I know.

I like Yossi and his family. They sit down and eat breakfast and dinner together, every day so far. Breakfast this morning is a selection of cheeses, yogurt, sliced tomatoes, toast and smoked salmon. No meat other than the salmon. The sun radiates warmth through the sliding glass doors from the balcony. Unlike my host in Tel Aviv, who lived in a cramped apartment block, Yossi's family lives in a hilltop home overlooking Haifa to the north and the nature reserve to the south. They are clearly wealthy—I've never been in a more luxurious home—and I'm finding that I'm distinctly uncomfortable with the surroundings. Yossi and Ramzy both have iPhones, only the second and third ones I've ever seen. Alex owns the first, yet another uncomfortable fact.

The great-grandmother, with her unpronounceable name and thick eastern European accent, asks, "What is on your agenda today?"

She's looking at me as she asks the question. She's been remarkably welcoming and kind since I've been here.

"We're going to be visiting a different high school," I say. "I can't remember the name."

"It's the Arab school," Yossi says.

Ramzy frowns, an angry expression on his face. "I don't see why they visit it at all."

Dana says to him, "Ramzy. How are the foreign exchange students supposed to learn anything if they don't get exposed to different places?"

The Arab school? I'm a little stuck on that.

Ramzy's response is bitter. "The only thing they need to know about the Arabs is that they are murderers."

Silence at the table. Painfully awkward silence. Politics never evokes this kind of emotion where I come from. I say, "I didn't realize there were separate schools for Arabs."

Dana says, "Yes. Arabs and Jews go to different schools in Israel."

"Even the Arab citizens?"

She nods.

"I don't think there should be Arab citizens," Ramzy says.

His great-grandmother says something sharp in Hebrew. Ramzy immediately drops his eyes and quiets down.

Dana looks sad. Then she says, in a quiet, toneless voice, "Dylan, you're probably not aware that my husband was murdered by a suicide bomber six years ago. The boys are... understandably bitter."

Jesus. The weight of that statement hits me hard.

"You probably never heard of the attack," Yossi said. "Hamas sent an *Arab* Israeli citizen to kill fellow citizens. He blew himself up at the train station in Nahariya. A hundred people were injured, and some killed. Our father was one. That was September 9, 2001."

"I'm so sorry for your loss," I say, automatically, flinching inside just a little at the mention of the date. The handsome man in the photo was killed in a suicide bombing. I kind of understand why they hadn't said much. It's one thing to say, "My parents are divorced," or even that one of them died. But this was a different level of complicated to explain.

Ramzy pushes his chin out, a pugnacious expression, as he says, "It's what Jews have to live with in this world. Betrayal. Killers within our own borders, who want us dead just because of who we are. And not just now but always. *Savta* will tell you, her whole family was murdered."

Savta is how the brothers refer to their great-grand-mother. She stirs and says, "It's true, my family died in one of the death camps. I was twelve when the camp was overrun, or I would have died too. But I tell you now, you must not hate. It will eat you alive, Ramzy."

I swallow. I'm not equipped to be involved in this discussion.

Dana echoes her grandmother. "Your father would never want to see you consumed with rage. He was a joyful man, and loved life."

"Yes, and look what happened to him," Ramzy says bitterly. He stands up and says to me, "You should ask them today, Dylan. Ask them if any of them would be suicide bombers. They should all be expelled to the Arab countries, and leave Israel to the Jews."

He stomps off. A grim silence falls over the family. I wish I could make myself invisible.

Dana looks at me and says, "Please forgive Ramzy."

"Of course," I say. But I can't help but think that the kind of hate Ramzy carries will just perpetuate the conflict. I've never been into politics, and I've never given even a moment's thought to the Arab-Israeli conflict. But being here, it is inescapable. It's everywhere. The conflict is in the memorials, which exist everywhere, the museums, and it is intertwined with the lives of everybody I've encountered.

Yossi sighs and says, "It's time to go."

We're quiet as we collect our things. I'm only carrying my backpack today, so I'm ready in just a moment, following Yossi and Ramzy out to the car. I was surprised to learn that their mother drives them to school every day—back home, I take the bus. But I learned yesterday that they stopped taking the bus to school after a bombing on a public bus in Haifa four years ago.

I sit in the back of the car, staring out the glass as Dana pulls the car out of their garage and onto the road. At some point in the last few days it started to sink in that there really isn't any distinction between the personal and the political. Back home I never thought of it really. Politics, policy, taxes, war—it's all very remote from the existence of a kid from an urban poor family. Mom certainly never talks about such things at home. But I couldn't even imagine what it must be like to have to change the way I go to school because of suicide bombers. Or to lose a family member to a bombing. Or to go to a school system where the *other* people go to school somewhere else.

Yossi sits next to me in the back seat—his younger brother up front with their mom. He starts to talk—not changing the subject, but talking more about the Palestinian-Israeli conflict. I just listen without responding. Part of me wants to just take a nap. I had a hard time sleeping last night—tossing and turning half the night. The thing is—this isn't a dream. I can't just turn it off and change the channel and go back home and everything goes back to normal. I wonder if this is what they mean when they talk about culture shock. Part of me wants to curl up into a ball somewhere.

But the other part of me is at the opposite end of the spectrum. Sometimes I'm elated at the experience, the emotions, the sheer overwhelming intensity of Alex. Other times I am just exhausted by the strangeness of it all.

Yesterday our group toured the Baha'ii Temple in Haifa, then met back up with our host students at the high school. We all went to the market in central Carmel after. Our host students, moving in a crowd, kept shouting at each other in Hebrew. *Everyone* in the market was shouting, and none of them spoke English except some of the shopkeepers who crooned, "American? German?" to the tourists who walked by.

But there is one saving grace in all of this chaos.

Alex.

Problem is... in less than three weeks... I have to say goodbye. And I'm falling for her, hard.

The thought of going home and leaving her?

It hurts.

I hate everyone (Alex)

The first thing I notice about the Arab school is that it hasn't been painted in what looks like many years.

This morning my host student, Lilah, warned me to expect things to be very different. Lilah's from Los Angeles—her family immigrated to Israel just one year ago. *Sometimes things are crazy here, Alex. You'll see. The first time we drove past the Arab school, I thought it was a jail.*

I can see why she thought it. Dylan and I get off the tour bus in front of the school, a huge cinderblock building in the center of Haifa. We're hand in hand. Dylan's been oddly quiet this morning—not that he's much of a conversationalist even under the best of circumstances, but when we get off the bus he mutters, "Separate but equal."

The cement blocks of the building were once painted blue. But that was a very long time ago. Lettering, painted next to the main entrance in Hebrew and Arabic, must be the name of the school. But nothing looks like it is being taken care of. The contrast to the modern new school Lilah attends is stark.

I squeeze Dylan's hand a little harder as the students gather in a circle around Mrs. Simpson. A man in his late forties stands next to her. He has dark curly hair and wears an open, collared shirt. He begins to speak, welcoming us to the school.

"I hope by the end of your visit that you'll have a little more understanding of the situation of Israeli Arabs," he says. Then he explains how this morning will be organized. We're going to go in groups of two to speak in each of the classes at the school for the next two hours. Then lunch in the main lunchroom with the Arab students.

Dylan leans close to me and whispers, "Did you know Yossi's father was killed by a suicide bomber?"

"Oh my God. No, I didn't know that."

"Crazy, ain't it? I can't imagine the… the rage it must take to do that."

I shrug. "I can't either," I whisper. "It's awful."

Then he says, "Change of subject. You look beautiful this mornin'."

I feel my skin flush, heat rushing from my cheeks down my neck. "Stop that," I whisper.

"Stop telling the truth? Why would I want to do that?"

Then he slips his arm around my waist.

Mrs. Simpson gives him a sour look. "Dylan...."

"Sorry, Mrs. Simpson," he says. Then he *winks* at her.

The crazy thing? She looks away, ignoring the wink. He's a rogue, a scoundrel. He's charming and kind and mischievous and ... he's mine.

But only for three more weeks.

The thought strikes me right through the heart. Because... I'm falling in love.

There's no doubt. Nothing else could explain the rush of heat I feel whenever I see him. The churning butterflies in my stomach... the lightheadedness I feel.

I love Dylan Paris.

I love him.

The words strike me with equal parts exhilaration and dread. Because the one thing I don't want to do is *say goodbye.*

Stop, Alex. Stop. You're *here* today.

My internal turmoil is interrupted when we all move into the school. Inside, the theme continues. The paint is actually peeling in many places. This building is at least fifty years old. The principal and Mrs. Simpson lead us through the school, dropping off pairs of students at each classroom.

Dylan and I go together. It's an all-girls class. The teacher approaches as we enter and holds out a hand. She has dark, almost black hair, and a smooth, light brown complexion with wide eyes. Her hair is tied up in some kind of complicated bun and she wears more formal clothing than is typical in Israel. Instead of jeans, she wears a long black dress with blue and red patterns on the front. "Good morning. I'm Marya Al-Marayati. Welcome, welcome." She has a broad smile as she says the words.

This is a fairly typical routine for us when we're speaking to a class. The idea is to tell the other kids about our lives, including ordinary details. I'm generally comfortable speaking in front of groups, so I haven't given it too much thought up until now. However, this is the first time I've shared a classroom with Dylan. It becomes painfully obvious, almost immediately, that he's more reticent in front of groups than he is one on one.

I try to help ease his transition by introducing myself first. Despite what my dad does for a living, my upbringing has really been fairly ordinary. I talk for a few minutes about living in China and Moscow, then what it was like to start school in San Francisco when my father finally retired.

Then Dylan begins to speak.

"My name's Dylan. I'm from Atlanta, Georgia. I get asked this a lot, since people don't know where it is, but Atlanta's in the southern United States, and it's where the 1996 Olympics were held. I turned 18 in June, but I'm still in high school because I started a year late. I haven't decided where I'm going to go to college, but I've been thinking about different options. I want to study writing. Which you can probably tell since I'm no good at speaking."

He says the last line with a lopsided grin and it evokes a laugh from the class.

Marya Al-Marayati says, "Girls, if any of you have questions, please raise your hand. Remember to introduce yourselves, please."

Several of the girls raise their hands. The teacher picks one, a tall girl with strong looking arms. The girl wears a gray cotton skirt and a white shirt. It would look like a school uniform, except the other girls are dressed in a wide variety of clothing.

She immediately launches into her question. "You come from America—what do people think of—"

Miss Al-Marayati interrupts. "Rania, introduce yourself, please."

The girl pauses and flashes a broad smile. "I'm Rania. It's nice to meet you. Can you tell me what students in the United States think of the conflict here?"

Dylan shifts uncomfortably. We meet each other's eyes, then he answers. "Honestly, most of the students I know don't think about it at all. They're like—teenagers anywhere I guess. A little self-absorbed. Interested in what's going on in their own lives."

Muttering seems to sweep across the classroom. I interject, "For most Americans, it seems so distant. I mean—we see news about it. I think everyone knows about the —"

I stop myself. Because I was about to say suicide bombings. But this is the Arab school.

Dylan doesn't seem to have the diplomacy I do. "Look—I wasn't part of the smart crowd at my school. So most of what I know is just conventional wisdom. And I hate to say it—but the conventional wisdom is that Arabs are terrorists. Americans are afraid."

Silence. Dead silence.

I swallow, then say, "That doesn't mean—"

The girl—Rania—interrupts me. "What do *you* think?" she says. "Are we all terrorists?" Her tone is belligerent.

"Of course not—" I say.

"Not you," she says. She doesn't even look at me. Her gaze—not friendly—is fixated on Dylan.

He says, "I expect you're probably not any different than I am. You like music, right? Do you hang out with your friends? Go out to eat? Go to the mall? It's not you and me that makes war. It's the crazies. The rest of us are just kind of along for the ride, right?"

Rania smiles. Then another girl raises her hand. The teacher points.

"Dylan, I'm Janine."

Why just Dylan? I wonder. I'm here too.

A second later I figure out the answer to that. The girl pauses, blushes, starts to speak, then blushes again. Two of the other girls giggle. Then Janine—petite, thin, big breasts—says, "How long are you staying in Haifa? And do you want to go dancing?"

Half of the girls burst into laughter. But I can tell Janine—who is a striking girl—is dead serious.

Dylan shakes his head and chuckles a little, then gives that stupid—and incredibly endearing—sideways grin of his. "I'd love to go dancing, but I'm already in love with a girl. I think I'll take her dancing instead. But thank you for the invite."

I'm already in love.

Did he just say that?

Did he say *I'm already in love?*

With me?

I feel lightheaded. I stand there, heat rushing up my cheeks. But then he looks at me. *He looks at me.* And I know he can see my face is red. He looks me dead in the eye. And what does he do?

He winks.

What the hell?

What does that mean?

Does it mean he was joking? He's not really *in love* with anyone? What is he playing some kind of game? Is this all some fun and games for him? He grins all the damn time, what's wrong with him?

Take a breath Alex. Get a grip.

I do. I take a breath, realizing that a third girl is asking yet another question of Dylan. I don't even catch the question, but it sounds like it is more nonsense, like *what does he do with his free time* and *are you on MySpace?*

I hate everyone.

Nothing but Drama (Dylan)

It's already dark when Yossi and I arrive at the Carmel Beach.

It's selfish of me, I guess, but I'm relieved Ramzy isn't along for the ride. We took the public bus here—it took almost an hour—and Ramzy is so depressing it's hard to know what to say around him. I have my guitar case slung over my shoulder.

We don't talk politics or war or the Palestinian/Israeli conflict on our way to the beach. Instead, we talk girls, a much more interesting topic. Here's what I learn: Yossi is very interested in a girl named Hannah. She's a junior, sixteenish (Alex's age) and she's really really pretty.

In actuality, I've met Hannah, because Hannah is Megan's host student. She's ... well... not all that pretty. Hawk nose, pinched little eyes, she looks angry. But Yossi doesn't see that—and he shouldn't. He clearly loves her. He spent *almost* the entire hour of the ride down to the beach talking about her. I know that she plays viola. I know her parents are sabras (a sabra is someone who was born in Israel, unlike most of the Israelis I've met who are either from Russia or the United States). I know she wants to go to school at the Technion and study microbiology.

Yossi also spends a lot of time questioning me about Alex. Questions I'm not really prepared to answer. Especially the most important one, the one he asked just as we were getting off the bus.

Do you love her?

I go kinda quiet after he asks that.

The thing is... I'll be honest. I *am* falling in love with her. She's everything I ever wanted in a girl, and then some. She's smart and cool and seriously freaking beautiful. In fact, she's more than what I've ever wanted—she's so much better than me that I hardly know what to think. Like, how can she *really* be interested in me? Is this just a short-term game? After all—we both agreed in advance, no long-term commitment here. This is a short-term relationship. We're here for a few weeks, then we go home, then we—

Don't see each other any more.

I don't want to think about going home.

I don't want to think about saying goodbye.

Jesus, Dylan. Get a hold of yourself. Almost three weeks left here. Why am I panicking already?

Instead of getting all weird about what's going to happen, I need to focus on appreciating what I have right now.

And it's moments after that thought hits that I see her.

A large group of high school students, both American and Israeli, are congregated on the beach. A fire is burning, illuminating them in flickering orange and yellow light. I can hear the waves crashing onto the beach, and a breeze blows in off the water. It's beautiful.

She's there. I see her, chatting in an animated fashion with Hannah—Yossi's girlfriend.

Yossi and I approach. Alex sees us first, and she meets my eyes, one perfectly arched eyebrow raised.

I'm no idiot. She caught my statement earlier, about how I'd fallen in love.

But how do you say that directly to someone you're going to lose anyway? There's no rules here. There's nothing that makes sense.

In any event, she stands and walks toward me. I find myself reaching for her hands as naturally as she reaches for mine, and then we're touching each other, eyes locked on each other. It's cool tonight, and she wears a thick sweater. My left hand slips down her right side and I can feel the firmness of her waist under the sweater.

"You were fantastic today," she whispers.

"So were you," I reply. "It's a miracle they didn't crucify me."

"It's a miracle they didn't kidnap you for sex."

The words shock me. "What? I don't—"

"Don't be an idiot, Dylan. That girl Janine? She practically tore her clothes off."

That's crazy, I think. Instead of saying that, though, I grip her hands a little tighter. "I can't even imagine. Except maybe with you."

She flushes a deep red, visible even in the failing light of the sunset. I lean forward and say, "I didn't mean to make you off balance, Alex. But I *do* want you to kiss me. Let's take a walk?"

She swallows visibly. *Is she nervous?* That's not even possible. I'm the one who is nervous. But all the same, we step away from the fire, and moments later we're engulfed in the darkness. The sound of the surf calms me, it gives me a strange confidence.

We hold hands as we walk, her right in my left. I try to figure out something... I don't know... normal? ... to say. I settle on a question. "How is your host family?"

She lets out a breath, as if she's been holding hers. Her shoulders actually lower a little. She *was* nervous. "I like them," she says. "Have you met Lilah?"

I shake my head.

"You can't miss her, I'll point her out when we get back. She's got ... a big personality. Wild curly hair."

"Wait... I think I did see her. Was she talking with Elle earlier? It looked like she had her cornered."

Alex laughs, hard. "Poor Elle. She gets nothing but flak."

"That's because she causes nothing but drama."

"True."

Alex turns toward the ocean and says, "God, it's beautiful here. You know Haifa reminds me a lot of home."

"San Francisco? Really?"

She nods. "I love it, really. It's beautiful. Colorful. I love the blues and the ocean breeze, and the best part is, my parents aren't here. For once in my life I get to be me. You know? Why the hell should I always have to be what they want? Why can't I be what I want for a change?"

As she says the words, she sounds bereft.

I pull her to me. "You don't have to be anyone with me but yourself, Alex."

She wraps her arms around me. "You mean it?"

"I mean it." I squeeze her a little tighter as I say the words. And right now, I mean it. I'd do anything at all for her. Anything. I want to tell her the words that catch in my throat, the words I'm afraid to say, the words that night ruin everything. Three simple words. *I love you.*

I don't say them. Instead, I hold her, and stare off to the horizon, and feel her warmth next to me.

I don't say them, but I think them. Over and over again. I try them on for size. In my head, I sing them. I whisper them. I shout them at the top of my lungs.

I love you, Alex Thompson.

CHAPTER TEN

Then there's Dylan (Alex)

'M INTOXICATED AS we walk back up the beach to rejoin the others. Drunk. High. Elated. I feel giddy, light-headed, excited. For the last—how long? Thirty minutes? An eternity?—Dylan and I have been on the beach, away from the others, side by side, kissing. Kissing so much my lips are sore. We hold hands comfortably, and I feel a warmth in his presence that I've never known before.

The fire is still blazing, but at least one thing has changed in our absence. First, a glass bottle of something has made an appearance and is being passed person to person. It has a medicinal smell, like gin. My first thought is to try some, but my second is to look at Dylan. He doesn't drink, and with plenty of good reasons. I'll wait.

One of the Israeli girls—I don't know her name—has taken out Dylan's guitar, which he left in its case when we walked off down the beach. At first I think he's going to be angry, but it doesn't seem to faze him. Instead, he stops walking and listens, a half smile on his face. He murmurs, "She's good."

A stab of jealousy rips through me, but I quickly suffocate it under a pillow. Keeping my face under the kind of plastic, strict control my diplomatic parents taught me, I say, "She is."

Lilah waves and I grab Dylan's arm and pull him away from the guitar-playing harpy.

"Hey, have you met Lilah? My host student?"

I more or less ignore Dylan's answer as I pull him over to that side of the fire. He has a somewhat bemused look on his face as we approach her.

"Hey, Lilah," Dylan says.

"Dylan! Thank God, someone real."

He chuckles. "Hardly that. What are you up to?"

She shrugs. "Just bumming around. You have no idea how happy I was when I found out I was going to be able to host a student."

Dylan and I sit down. He leans against a bench, and I lean against him and look at Lilah. She's my age, and she's from California, but that's where our similarities come to an end. She's tiny, with jet-black hair, giving her an appearance almost like my sister Sarah, but without all the spikes and weird colors. I bet the two of them would get along just fine. Lilah has her eyes heavily made up, with cats' eyes drawn on with black eyeliner.

"How come?" he asks.

Lilah says, "Let me count the reasons. I don't speak Hebrew worth a damn. I miss Burger King and Starbucks and American accents." She leans close to us both. Her eyes dart around us as if checking who is close by. But she doesn't blink. She scoots closer to us and whispers, "And I hate it here. I hate my parents for bringing me here."

"Yeah?" Dylan says.

"You would too. Leaving everything you know to go colonize someone *else's* country? Mom and Dad are trying to get a spot in one of the Settlements. They're crazy. It'll be awesome. Live in a crowded apartment on land stolen from some poor farmer, surrounded by people who hate us and not-so-well-protected by the Army that I'll be forced to join in just two years? That's the best thing I've ever heard."

I swallow. "That's not how the rest of the kids here seem to describe it."

Lilah shrugs. "Of course not. They're rats inside the trap. I bet every single one of them knows someone who was injured or killed in the last uprising. So they hate. The Palestinians hate. Even my parents hate, and they're from fucking Santa Ana. Want to see how much good hating does anyone? Go look at the aftermath of one of the bombings. Or an apartment block that's been blown up because one asshole from Hamas decided to hide in the basement, no matter how many kids live there."

A voice behind me almost makes me jump. It's Yossi, Dylan's host student. "And that, Lilah, is why we don't date anymore. You'd rather hand our home to the Palestinians than defend it. You should go home."

Yossi and Lilah dated? I didn't realize.

Lilah replies in a fierce voice, "Trust me, I would if I could. I'll be on a plane the day I turn eighteen."

"*Sheket!* Crazy bitch." Yossi storms off. What an ass.

Lilah sighs. Dylan looks worried.

I ask the most important question. "You two used to date?"

"Yeah," she says, her tone wistful.

"It's hard not to blame him for his reaction," Dylan says.

I think about what Dylan told me this morning—Yossi's father killed by a suicide bomber. "I guess if my father had been killed that way, I'd hate too."

"There was a big war going on here, then," Lilah says. "I've read about the bombing that killed Yossi's father. 94 people were wounded, four killed. The thing was, it wasn't even a Palestinian from the territories who did it. It was an Arab-Israeli—a citizen."

I feel Dylan shake his head. "All the more reason to be angry."

Lilah's expression is fierce. "No. No, it's not. You don't see it. It just gets worse and worse. Each side gets worse weapons, commits worse atrocities, and blames the other side for their part in it. The Palestinians lob missiles into Israel, or send suicide bombers who blow up buses and children and weddings, and the Israelis send fighter jets and blow up apartment blocks, or bulldozers to destroy people's homes, or walls to separate them from their land."

Dylan looks doubtful. But the thing I notice is that the eyes of *all* the Israeli students are now on us. Which doesn't mean we should stop talking about it, but seriously, couldn't she have a little discretion?

But then the craziest thing happens. Lilah's eyes suddenly water as they fix on some spot behind me. I twist around and see it.

Yossi. He and Hannah are walking off into the darkness with a girl. I think it's Megan's host student… I don't know her name. But Lilah clearly knows her.

Her face shifts into a frown and she says, "I need to get going soon, Alex. Are you coming with me?"

Oh, no. I'm suddenly painfully torn. I can imagine how Lilah must feel right now. And she *is* my host-student, which means I pretty much have to go home with her. It's not like I'll be able to find my way to her house on my own.

But I don't want to leave Dylan.

Lilah stares at me, waiting for an answer. The answer I don't have.

Dylan breaks the impasse in his calm southern accent. "It's okay, Alex. I don't mind, and it looks to me like Lilah could use some company. Lilah, can you give us a few moments?"

I sigh. I can't decide what I like the most about Dylan. But his concern for others is near the top of the list. Most of the guys I know? They're utterly self-centered. Not just the teenagers, but even the adults I come into contact with. My whole life has been a procession of self-centered, self-seeking people who only look for what they want to get out of other people.

And then there's Dylan. He's nothing like any guy I've ever known. And sometimes I think he's unlike any guy I ever *will* know.

What will I do when it's time to go home?

Sorry, man (Dylan)

Back before I started to try to get my life together, I used to do a fair amount of drugs. Nothing heavy, except once or twice, but I smoked more than my share of pot and drank way too much. It's why I'm so militantly against drinking now, because despite that initial high, the after effect was always nothing but grief.

Tonight, though, as we catch the bus back to Yossi's neighborhood, I feel almost as if I'm high. I'm lightheaded, and all I can think about is Alex. I ended up playing guitar for a little while, then passed the guitar off to one of the other students who knew how to play. I really wanted to just have my arms around Alex. Holding her, I was content in a way I'd never experienced. Once she was gone, I was restless and ready to go.

I don't talk much at all on the bus ride back. Yossi doesn't seem to mind—he takes out his expensive phone and plays a game on it while we ride the bus. I think he's still angry about Lilah. It's a little after ten at night when we get back to the house.

Yossi's mother is still awake and has guests, three other women. They're sitting around the living room talking and drinking. Yossi's mother throws her head back and laughs. For just a second, she looks twenty years younger, and it sinks in again how incredibly painful the loss of her husband must have been.

Yossi walks to his mother and kisses her on the top of her head. Then, very polite, he introduces me to the other three women. A moment later we're headed back to his room.

"Mind if I use the computer?" I ask.

He waves a hand in assent. "I'm going to go take a shower."

I switch the computer on and wait for it to boot up while he gathers up his things and steps out of the room. I don't know why, but I've got this anxious feeling coming on, a tight feeling in my chest. It's been a week since I messaged Scott looking for her. I've only been online once since then, and he hadn't responded then.

But tonight, the Inbox link has a number 2 beside it. I've got two messages. I click on the link.

The first message is from Alex. The second from Scott.

I take a deep breath. I start to click on Scott's message—but then stop at the last second and click on Alex's instead.

It says,

I had a great time at the beach tonight. I know we only have a few weeks, but I'm so happy we get to spend that time together. I know you don't think so, Dylan, but you're really a great guy. You're kind and sweet and considerate. You treat me better than any boy I've ever dated. I wish I could introduce you to my sisters! I know they would love you.

I haven't been able to say it, but I'm dreading going home. When I think of my life at home, compared to now, it all seems colorless and sad.

Thank you for being my friend,

xo xo xo

Alex

I close my eyes, letting her words sink in, thinking of kissing her tonight on the beach, thinking of the fullness of her lips, the curve of her waist. She wrote *xo xo xo*. That's... significant? I love her. I haven't told her yet, but I love her.

I sigh and open my eyes. Then I click into Scott's message.

Dylan, dude. Sorry, man. Spot's dead.

As soon as I read the words, I gasp and my eyes water. *She's dead? How? When?* It's been almost a year since I last saw her, a year since I saved myself and left her behind. A year since she disappeared. *What happened? Why didn't Scott give me any details?*

Grief and rage I've never experienced in my life flood through me. She was dead because her parents kicked her out, because they couldn't accept her for who she was. Instead of loving their daughter, they'd pushed her out into a world that did horrible things to young women on their own.

A wave of images of my friend. Spot laughing, a deep laugh that seemed to start near her toes, rocking her body as she leaned back, eyes wide. Spot on her first day at her attempt at a job, wearing a silly uniform with a bow tie and serving ice cream. She got fired because they changed her schedule and there was no number to call her, and she didn't know the schedule had changed. She cried that night—Spot had wanted off the streets, and thought the job might get her there.

I had known better, even then. No minimum wage job was going to be enough to pay for a place to live.

I had been so afraid. Afraid, because she was a young, pretty girl. Whether or not she was a lesbian wouldn't turn off a rapist or a pimp. I'd looked at her as a little sister, and would have done anything to protect her.

Anything but stay on the streets myself. I'd chosen to go back to school, to move back home, and she disappeared before I could do anything to help her.

I close my eyes and wrestle my face into something resembling calm. I don't want to have to answer questions. I don't want to have to tell Yossi about Spot. I turn off the computer. I climb to the upper bunk, still in my clothes, and roll over, turning my back to the room. When Yossi comes back in, I pretend I'm asleep.

But I don't sleep. Instead, I remember Spot the last time I saw her. It wasn't fair. She'd done nothing wrong. She didn't deserve to be pushed out on her own. She didn't deserve to be alone.

At that moment, I make a promise to myself. A promise that I'll never let someone helpless go unprotected. I've always wanted to be a writer, but in that moment I feel the urge to change directions. To become … a cop, or a firefighter, a social worker, even a soldier. Somebody who protects and helps others.

I can't believe she's dead.

Hours pass before I fall asleep.

CHAPTER ELEVEN

In'shallah (Alex)

WHEN WE GATHER outside the high school this morning, Dylan is standing off to the side smoking a cigarette, away from everyone else. It's a pale, washed-out sunrise, long shadows and blue-black darkness seeming to hide distasteful emotions.

Normally Dylan is wide awake, alert. He paces around. He fidgets. His eyes are everywhere. But today? Today he just stands, staring into the distance. He doesn't even notice me. Was it something I did?

"Hey," I say quickly. I've got a tight feeling in my stomach.

He jerks a little, but recovers quickly.

"Mornin'," he drawls.

"You okay?" I ask.

"Sure," he says. He shrugs. "Tired. You?"

I reach out to take his hand. He takes it, but a fraction of a second slower than usual. Something really is going on. I run through the day before in my mind. Maybe it was something I did or said at the beach party last night? I'm sure he'll tell me—if not soon, then at least when we're on the bus. We have a longer trip today, visiting sites in Nazareth and around the Sea of Galilee, or, as the Israelis call it, Lake Kinneret. I can be patient.

I don't press. Not even as we board the bus, and the chaperones call the roll to make sure we are all there, and the bus departs Haifa.

But what if it's something awful? I left the party before he did. Did something happen? Is he—am I—?

Stop.

I tell myself to get a grip. He'll talk about it, whatever it is.

The drive to Nazareth from Haifa is less than an hour, winding through largely-urban areas, traffic circles and Arabic and Hebrew lettering everywhere. But it seems a lot longer, because Dylan leans against the window, staring out. He's quiet. I don't nag him. Something's obviously wrong, and I presume he'll tell me eventually. In the meantime, we sit together and hold hands quietly.

The urban neighborhoods give way to dusty hills, the few bare trees looking like invaders. Orange traffic signs, all of them marked in three languages, alternate with signs which I can barely guess the meaning of, despite the fact that I've lived in a lot of different countries.

Nazareth is a city of hills. A riot of colors, languages, fragrances.

Graffiti I can't understand covers walls beside the road. A giant yellow frowny face holds a stop sign with Arabic lettering, next to words I don't understand. People wait at the bus stop near the frowny-face, huddled over, wearing jackets against the pending chill which is expected to set in later today.

A block later, a small cafe—lettering in Arabic only, except the large Coca-Cola sign—with green plastic lawn furniture out front. Four elderly men sit at the plastic table. A few blocks later, a computer store next to a convenience store next to a parking deck next to a park. No—not a park. A cemetery. A few doors down from there, a vegetable market spills out into the street, crates of colorful lettuce, oranges and other unidentifiable vegetables piled up in and outside the market. A voice whispers that there's something wrong with the fact that I don't recognize half of these plants or even know if they are edible. I grew up knowing how to order in French at fancy restaurants, but I can't cook much more than boxes of macaroni and cheese. And I'm regretting that. I want to know more.

The bus finally stops on a crowded, narrow street on a hill, double-parked and blocking traffic. . The bus driver gets out just as a shopkeeper boils out of his shop, rage on his face. The two men stand there, in the street for several minutes, waving their arms, shouting at each other in Arabic. Dylan watches them, but not with any level of interest. Finally his eyes just wander off.

What is wrong with him? If he doesn't start talking soon, I'm going to get very bent out of shape.

The argument outside seems to quiet down, and finally, the bus driver steps back on board the bus. In his thickly accented English, he says to Mrs. Simpson, "Here. The guide will be here in fifteen hour."

"I'm sorry, what?"

The driver closes his eyes, as if consulting an inner dictionary. Then he says, "*Soon.* The guide will be here soon. *In'shallah.*"

That phrase I recognize. *God Willing.* In this context, it generally indicates that the speaker isn't sure of when something is going to happen, or even if it will happen at all.

Whether or not the guide is coming seems to be an open question. In the meantime, we pile off the bus.

The neighborhood we are in is clearly a regular tourist stop. Shops line both sides of the street—souvenirs, cameras, phones, gifts. The next block over is another vegetable market, crates and boxes piled high, blocking the sidewalk, with a riot of colors and fragrances.

Mrs. Simpson gathers us into a circle. "I don't know when the guide will be here, so I'm going to give you thirty minutes. Stay on this block, and feel free to walk around, but I want you to stay in pairs."

Freedom. It's unusual that we get to just walk around even for a short time—most of our stops have been guided, scripted and led every step of the way.

We walk in a small group—John and Elle, who seem to be tolerating each other's company again, and me and Dylan. Elle keeps up a continual patter of talk, which obscures the fact that Dylan is completely silent. He's not typically the most talkative of people anyway—the others don't seem to notice his mood.

We're walking on foot through a market of a completely different culture, and yet Dylan looks around with no interest at all.

Around us is a scene that I suspect is both timeless and yet very tied to the tourist trade. The strong aroma of spices drifts out of a building. We look in to see large vats and bags of spices. Cinnamon, cloves, ginger, paprika and more, bright colors spilling out of open containers. Just beyond the spice shop is a tourist shop—John buys himself a kuffeyah, the traditional black-and-white checkered headdress worn by Arab men. Then he buys a bracelet for Elle. It's not a terribly expensive bracelet, but all the same, I get a sinking feeling. Dylan has a lot more pride than money (or sense).

He looks in the jewelry case the bracelet came from. He hides his expression, but I see his eyes widen just a little bit. Most of it is handmade in silver.

"Dylan, can we grab some coffee?" I ask, desperate to distract him. "I'm not feeling well."

At my words, he immediately shifts his attention to me. "What's wrong?"

I shake my head. "I just didn't get enough sleep. Do you mind?"

"Of course not," he says. We take each other's hands and walk out of the shop.

Different worlds (Dylan)

I don't mean to be an ass, but I know that Alex is upset. She hasn't asked me what's wrong, but it is obvious she wants to know. . But I don't know what to tell her. So I just kind of shove all of that to the side and keep going.

But the effort of shoving my grief aside leaves me feeling nothing at all, not even the heady, intoxicating emotions I normally feel around Alex. And that's not okay.

So I walk through the market with her, holding hands. I feel outclassed, outmatched, when John buys a bracelet for Elle. She's thrilled, I can see it, and she hugs him with a little squeal. I do a quick mental calculation of how much money I have left for this trip (not much), and look into the cabinet. And gulp. The cheapest item in the cabinet is 400 shekels... about a hundred dollars.

That's more than I even have to last me for the remaining time we're in Israel. Then Alex says she doesn't feel well, and asks if we can get a cup of coffee.

I'm not an idiot. I can see that she put everything together very quickly, and is now rescuing me from myself.

I have to accept the lifeline because there's no choice. So we walk out of the store and down the street, where we take a seat at a sidewalk cafe.

"I loved the smells in the spice market," she says. I think she's stretching to come up with something to say.

I don't know what to say. So I nod, and say, "Yeah, I like it here."

A waiter comes out, crooning, "Hello, English? German?"

"American," Alex says.

"American! You know George Bush!"

"No," I say, making a bit of a sour face. Then I find myself wondering if Alex actually has met him. We both ask for coffee, and the waiter swoops off.

I lean forward. "So... *do* you know George Bush?"

She sticks her tongue out at me. Then says, "I met him once, when I was twelve."

When she stops speaking, I say, "Come on, Alex. Is that it? You met him once? Where? At the beach? The golf course? What?"

She laughs, then says, "If you must know, it was a formal dinner at the White House. My Dad was going on some diplomatic thing, I think to Iraq. I'd never been invited to anything like that before. I thought he was a nice man. He laughed a lot."

"That's wild." I shake my head. "You know, we come from completely different worlds."

She says, "It doesn't matter."

"Doesn't it though? I mean… sometimes I wonder if we can really understand each other."

"Of course we can." Her eyes show a flash of hurt as she says the words.

I lean forward and take her hand. "It's okay, Alex. I'm sorry. It just means we have to reach a little further, that's all."

"What's wrong with you today?" Her tone isn't angry. But it carries an urgency to it.

I swallow. Then I tell her about Spot.

Are we getting serious? (Alex)

As Dylan tells me the story of his friend Spot, I feel a growing sadness. He stumbles over his words, at one point just going completely silent.

"Anyway," he says. "I never saw her again. But when I set up my Facebook account after we met, and I connected almost immediately with some people from high school, I guess I thought I might be able to use it to find her. But..."

His expression is so bleak, I'm terrified of what he's going to say. I squeeze his hand.

"I found out last night ... one of the guys ... he says she's dead."

"Oh my God. What happened?"

He shakes his head, his face somber. "No idea. I asked, but he hasn't answered. But ... I mean... it's not safe out there on the street. For anyone, but especially for girls."

I squeeze his hand again. This is awful, and I hardly know what to say to him. Maybe he's right. Maybe there are things we just can't understand about each other, because we come from different worlds. Maybe I don't know what it's like to lose a friend that way.

But I can still be there for him — and he can for me. I lean forward, taking his other hand in mine so that I'm holding both of his. I look in his eyes. "You can talk to me, you know. I may not have lived the life you have, but I care. I *care*."

He shifts uncomfortably, "Alex, I can't dump all my problems on—"

"Stop. That's what people do. They take care of each other. You did your best to take care of your friend, and I admire you for that. Well, now it's my turn to take care of you. All right?"

He shudders. "I'm not used to depending on anybody."

"Maybe it's time you got used to it."

"It's not that easy."

I smile. "Nothing worth doing is that easy."

He stares at me, slowly shaking his head. "Are we getting serious?"

"What does that mean?" I ask. Suddenly my heart is pounding. Because I haven't told him. That I love him. How can I, when we're going home in the blink of an eye? But I want to. I want to tell him, loud and clear: Dylan, I love you.

He swallows, and mutters, "I don't know."

"Let's just let it be what it is, Dylan. We don't have to give it words. We know what we feel."

He nods. "Right. We just ... let it happen."

He looks so uncomfortable, I'm not sure what to say. So I don't say anything. Instead, I stand and give him a kiss on the cheek. Then I return to my seat.

"That's it?" he asks.

I grin. "For now."

His eyes widen. "Wait... I thought..."

"Well... yes... I'm waiting. Until I marry."

He sighs. Then we both laugh. For now at least, we're okay.

A few hours later. We're standing on the Golan Heights, overlooking the Sea of Galilee. I've got a scarf around my face because of the fierce wind that buffets our clothes. A speaker from the nearby kibbutz is talking about security problems and suicide bombers and the threat from Syria, just across the border. But neither I nor Dylan really pay attention.

Instead, we're wrapped up, staring in each other's eyes. I find his touch reassuring—and one of us is constantly touching the other. As the crowd of students shifts away from us, Dylan leans in close and says, "I need to kiss you right now."

I whisper, "If you need to, then, I guess you should go ahead."

He does.

Chapter Twelve

Dear Mom (Dylan)

FROM: DylanParis81@gmail.com
TO: LovelyLinda1969@aol.com
SUBJECT: (no subject)
Dear Mom:
I'm writing from Haifa, which is a coast city in Israel. The town mostly sprawls on a mountain overlooking the Mediterranean Sea. It's truly beautiful here. Sometimes I feel like I've left reality entirely. Back home I'm the kid who dropped out of school and smoked too much pot and drank too much. Here, I'm — one of the smart kids. Just like everyone else. Except I often feel out of place. Like I've snuck into a party full of rich people, and I have to figure out the right kinds of manners to use.

The good news, Mom, is that you prepared me pretty well for this, just as you did for everything else. I know we've had our moments, our conflicts. But don't ever think I don't know how much you've sacrificed for me.

Anyway.

I'm mostly writing to tell you about Spot. Do you remember her? Her parents had kicked her out because she was gay. She was like a little sister, if I'd ever had one. I found out from Scott—one of the guys I used to hang out with, unfortunately—that she's dead. I don't know how or why or what happened, but I can imagine it. Drug overdose, or maybe she was murdered. There were always guys out there, predators who caught sight of a teenage girl on the streets and wanted—well, you know.

I'm not gonna lie, Mom. I'm heartbroken. She was my friend, and I feel like I failed. I wasn't there for her, I wasn't there to protect her. I know I had to get off the street and clean up my act, and I don't have any regrets. But ... it hurts to know that she's gone.

Anyway. What else? We leave for Jerusalem tomorrow. It still doesn't even seem real to me. A couple days ago we walked through a building they believe was occupied by the first generation of Christians two thousand years ago. I really want to learn more about this part of the world, about all this history. I've thought about coming back when I finish high school, maybe for a few months or a year, before I start college. I'd love to be able to really sink my teeth into this place.

I know that's probably not the news you wanted to hear. I *will* go to college, I promise.

In the meantime. Can I tell you about Alex?

Hah. I knew I'd surprise you with something. I met a girl. She's ... beautiful. Smarter than I am, by a long shot. She speaks a fair amount of Chinese and Russian and lived in both countries. Her dad's a diplomat. She's — amazing. Honestly—I haven't told her this yet. But I think I love her.

I don't think. I *do* love her.

Problem is... she lives in San Francisco. She's only sixteen, doesn't graduate high school for another year and a half. Her life is… headed in a different direction. Maybe. I don't know. She says she's still trying to decide between Harvard and Columbia. Crazy, huh? Her older sisters went to those schools. I'll be lucky if I can get into Georgia State.

All the same, as much as I miss you—and I miss you a lot—I am dreading going home. I'm dreading saying goodbye. It's going to be at least two years before we can be together—if ever. That feels like an eternity. It is an eternity.

Would you ever forgive me if I asked Alex to run away with me?

I know. You're always practical. That's part of what I love about you.

Mom—thanks for everything. It won't be long at all before I'm home. Please forgive me if I'm not as happy to be home as I ought to be. Because inside, when I say goodbye to Alex, I'll be dying.

I love you,
Dylan

A guy? A girl? (Alex)

As I listen to a series of clicks and hisses after I dial the number, I find myself simultaneously irritated that it's taking so long to place the call and exasperated with myself that I'm irritated. After all, I'm placing a direct dial call from my phone, in my pocket, with its San Francisco phone number, to another phone in Vienna, even though *that* phone originated in Boston. By all rights, it *ought* to take a long time to place that call.

Instead, it took twenty seconds, tops, before I heard Julia's line begin ringing.

"Hello?" she said a moment later.

A little background here. I think I've mentioned that my sister Julia is twenty-five, the oldest of my sisters. She's also the only one who is married. Her husband, Crank, is an alternative rock/punk guitarist and singer. Picture: family holidays with my uptight-as-hell parents, with their son-in-law Crank flourishing his bright green mohawk and gleaming eyebrow piercings.

They don't make reality TV that entertaining.

"Julia? It's Alex."

"Hey, little sister. What are you doing? Aren't you in Israel?"

I smile. It doesn't matter what's going on, Julia and Carrie are almost always ready to drop everything to talk with me. I'm grateful for it. Sometimes it's tough being at home with Mom and dealing with all of her emotional ups and downs. Sometimes tough, as a word, is inadequate.

"I am," I reply. "In Haifa."

"Beautiful city," she says. "Crank and I were there last summer for a concert. It reminds me a lot of San Francisco."

"Me too," I say.

Just then the door to the bedroom opens and Lilah walks in. "Oh!" she says. "Are you on the phone?"

I nod. She backs out. Lilah has been excessively po-lite and considerate since the outbursts the other night at the beach, as has her ex-boyfriend Yossi. Dylan reports that politics has been ruled too sensitive to discuss in the house for the remainder of our visit. Which is disappointing, really. We're here to learn. But it seems like everyone's afraid we'll learn too much.

"So what's going on?" Julia asks. "Is everything okay? How is the trip?"

I sigh. "It's good. Wonderful, actually."

"Oh, yeah?"

"Well, see... there's...." I trail off.

"A guy? A girl?" she asks.

I chuckle. "A guy."

"Okay. What about him?"

"It's a long story. His name's Dylan, and ... Julia, I really like him. A lot."

"Like?"

"Well. Julia." I whisper. "I love him."

"That's so exciting!" Julia says.

"But that's not why I called."

"No?"

"Listen. You *can't* tell Mom. I'm serious. You can't tell her *anything.*"

"My lips are sealed. You know that."

I sigh. Of course I know that. Even ten years later, the war between Mom and Julia is legendary. I was little when she left, but I still remember some of it. The two of them are on speaking terms now, but I doubt they'll ever be close. I don't see how *anyone* can be close to our mom.

"Okay. See, the thing is... Dylan is not exactly from the same kind of background as us. He's... from a poor family. He dropped out of high school for a while. Got into drugs. He was even living out on his own for a while."

In a droll tone, Julia said, "Alex, this is all very shocking."

That makes me chuckle. Everything I've just said could also be said of Crank. "Okay. I knew you'd understand."

"He's cleaned up his act?" she asks.

"Yes. And he's... Julia... he's good. He doesn't know it, but he's really kind. But that's not why I called."

Julia laughs. "Are you *ever* going to get to why you called? I'm not in any hurry, I don't hear from you often enough."

"I am," I say. "You just needed that background. I'm ready."

"Okay."

"Dylan had this friend. When he was living on the street. She went by the street name of Spot—he doesn't know what her actual name is. He said she was fourteen at the time... which makes her about sixteen now."

"Okay...." Julia's voice trails off.

I swallow. "Spot got kicked out of her house because she was gay. And for a while they were close friends. He says she was like a sister to him. But when he cleaned up and went back to school, she disappeared. He tried to find her, but no luck. Anyway... a mutual friend of theirs told Dylan the other night that Spot is dead."

Julia mutters a barely audible curse.

"Anyway... that's the story. The thing is... we don't know when it happened... or what happened... or why.

And … Dylan's really broken up about it, Julia. She really was a little sister to him, I can see it. He loved her. I want to find out who she was, and what happened to her."

"And… how can I help?"

I smile, just a little. "I just… can I borrow some money?" I swallow, then launch into my pitch. "Like… a few thousand dollars? Mom or Dad would never help with this. But I'm thinking, maybe a private detective, or something like that, could find out something. There can't be that many teenage girls turning up… dead… in Atlanta. Can there? It seems like we should be able to track her down. At least then Dylan could have some idea what happened to his friend."

Silence at the other end of the line. I breathe, then a little faster, then I say, too quickly, "Julia, I can pay you back. I really can. I don't get my trust fund until I'm 21 but I'll get a part time job somewhere, or—"

"Alex, stop." Her command is sharp. "It's not that. I'd gladly pay whatever you need," she says.

"You'll help? Really?"

"Alex—are you sure you want to get mixed up in this? Does he mean that much to you?"

I sniff. *Damn it.* I wasn't going to get emotional. But I can't help myself. "Julia, you didn't see his eyes. He's so sad."

"And you want to take care of him."

Horrified at myself, I hiccup. "Yes. He's got a strength I've never seen. But it's buried under a lot of pain. Julia, you'd love him. Please help?"

"Of course. Tell me everything you know about her. Where were they? You said Atlanta? I know a guy there, lawyer for one of the studios... he might know some people. How long are you going to be in Haifa?"

"We leave for Jerusalem in the morning, then back to the United States on December 9th."

"Oh... you don't have much time left at all."

When she says that, I almost feel tears welling up again. "No," I whisper.

"Chin up, Alex. You can handle this. If it's the real thing, I promise you it will survive some time and distance."

She's right. Besides, I graduate high school in another 18 months. That's not long at all when you consider everything. Maybe we can go to college together? Maybe...

It's too early to think about all that. Way too early.

But I love him.

I swallow. Then I start telling Julia everything I can remember.

CHAPTER THIRTEEN

A view from forever (Dylan)

FOR FOUR WEEKS, Alex and I have been riding on buses together all over the country. We've been in Tel Aviv and Haifa, Nazareth and the Dead Sea. But *this* ride, to Jerusalem, is the quietest we've been. We've ridden the two-hour drive mostly in silence, her leaning against me, both of us sometimes looking out at the countryside and mostly at each other. About halfway through the ride I kissed her, all of my attention zeroed down to the scent of her hair (strawberry) and the pliable, wet feel of her lips against mine.

After a few moments of that, I hear a disapproving throat clearing. We break apart, in a bit of a haze, only to see Mrs Simpson in the seat in front of us. She's sort of towering over us, actually.

"I'm well aware you two are in love. But please maintain some decorum in the bus." She gives me a kind smile, then steps away, leaving me and Alex sitting there, heat on our faces.

I'm well aware you two are in love.

I haven't told Alex that, have I? No. Not yet. But it's true. There's no doubt. Loving her is ... it's ecstasy. It's intoxicating, it feels like I'm gently floating up into the sky holding her hands. But it's also agony. It's knowing that I have to say goodbye. It's knowing that in 8 days, we get on a plane back to the United States and we might not ever see each other again. It *hurts*.

We both sink back into our seat. I look at her with a grin, and she smiles back. Neither of us says anything. But I take her right hand in my left, and she leans her head on my shoulder. We ride a few more minutes, and then she says, "Dylan? Will you play me a song?"

I swallow. Then I nod. She shifts off my shoulder, and I stand and pull my guitar down from the overhead rack and open the case. Quickly I tune the instrument.

I close my eyes, centering myself. I feel a tightness in my chest, my heart beating loud enough I can hear the pulse in my ears even over the bus. Because I haven't played this song for her. Because, well, I hadn't written it until the other night. Usually I just play covers, mostly old folk and southern rock—Eagles, Dylan (of course), Atlanta Rhythm Section, Cat Stevens. But this one is *mine*. But that's not the reason I'm struggling a little. The reason for that is because it's about *her*.

I take a breath, then strum an open E chord, followed by a slow A Minor. Then I begin to work my way through the song. The beginning is all guitar, no lyrics. I was going for a haunting, almost ethereal sound, with occasional harmonics.

Her eyes are directly on me. So I start singing.

Broken
Lost
Alone
A boy lost in forever
Out on his own

Afraid
Determined
Driven
A boy rebuilding a life
But heart still hidden

Her eyebrows are drawn together, her eyes on me. I think she was expecting me to play something familiar. If so, this has caught her by surprise. I shift to a new key for the chorus.

But then a new day came
A desert, a sea, a sky, a love
But then a new day came
Everything changed

Back to the original key for the next two verses.

Magic
Beauty
Brilliance
A girl from forever
He found her

A touch
An embrace
A kiss
He wanted her to know
What he couldn't say with words

At this point, I'm looking out the window, because *I can't* look at her. *I can't.* Not with what I'm about to sing. But I keep going, because I don't know what the hell else I'm supposed to do.

But then a new day came
Adore
worship
idolize
treasure

But then a new day came
Because the boy had found what he'd always needed,
what he'd always wanted
A view from forever

With the last word of my sappy as hell song, I strike a power chord F that rings through the whole bus with a resounding hum. I don't hear any response—or see any, because, my eyes are squeezed shut.

But then someone in the back starts clapping. I open my eyes, and hear more of them, all of the kids on the bus clapping.

Alex, though, she stares at me. Green eyes wide, the faintest, most beautiful smile on her face.

I can feel heat on my cheeks. "I... um... cobbled that one together the other night." Stumbling on my words, I open up my guitar case. Then drop it. I pick it up again and put the guitar in, my cheeks hot. I snap the case shut and toss the guitar back up top. And cough.

Finally I sit back down, and pray for the bus trip to continue.

That song (Alex)

That song.

Was he really singing about me? He was. He was singing to me. About me. *He wrote a song about us.*

Dylan hasn't said *I love you.* But he wrote a song about me.

I'm hyperventilating.

As the other students stop clapping, I whisper, "That was beautiful."

He just shrugs, a faint smile on his face. He's nervous. I can see it. Normally confident as hell, Dylan's vulnerable side comes out when it comes to showing who he is deep inside. I make it easy on him. I lean forward and kiss him hard on the lips. Mrs. Simpson can just close her eyes and look away.

Unfortunately, the rest of the kids burst into applause again at our kiss.

Now *I'm* the one who is blushing.

Half an hour later the bus arrives in Jerusalem. Unlike Haifa, which looked a lot like home, and Tel Aviv, which looks almost generic with its glass and steel towers, Jerusalem is firmly a city out of the ancient world. Our route into the city initially takes us through winding and sparse desert hills, great ravines to either side of the highway. We start to come into the suburbs, but we're trapped in urban traffic. Cars and pedestrians everywhere. The buildings almost all of the same dun-colored stone. Palm trees scattered here and there.

All of us crane our necks to get a good look out of the bus. People everywhere, some of them dressed in normal western clothing, others in green uniforms—many, many uniforms—others in the black suits, beards and hats of the ultra-Orthodox Hasidic Jews. The street signs are trilingual—Hebrew, Arabic and English. Normally, men and women with uniforms and guns are everywhere in Israel, but they are far more evident in Jerusalem. On every street corner.

Mrs. Simpson stands up and says, "Our driver says we'll shortly see the walls of the Old City. Then we'll be headed to the King David Hotel for a diplomatic luncheon. You will all want to be on your best behavior, because the British Ambassador will be giving a speech."

"That will be just as exciting as watching snow melt on a cold day," I mutter.

Dylan snickers. "To you, maybe. It'll all be brand new to me."

I shrug. Then I sit up straight. "Look!" I say.

Just overhead in front of the bus, green street signs. One on the left says, "Damascus Gate." The one on the right reads, "Jaffa Gate/Talpiyot." Ahead, between the rows of buildings, a large stone wall with stone towers. The wall grows as we approach. It has crenellated battlements, and rising above the wall are church steeples and minarets.

"The Old City," Dylan says. "I *so* want to go there."

"Me too," I say. "Do you think they'll let us?"

"I don't know. There's supposed to be an official tour next Thursday. But I'm not sure about non-official visits."

The bus turns right when we reach the old city and begins to circumnavigate the city. The walls are beautiful, and huge, towering over the hundreds of people we see walking everywhere.

I grab Dylan's hand without thinking, pulling it to my lap. Next Thursday will be close to our last day in Jerusalem. I don't want to think that far ahead. I don't want to think to the time I have to say goodbye.

Half an hour later, the bus has made it through the traffic and we arrive in front of the King David Hotel. A multi-story building made of the same tan stone as everything else in the city, it's fronted with tall trees and a lot of greenery. The bus stops at the sidewalk, not attempting to navigate the curved driveway. We all stay aboard as Mrs. Simpson steps off the bus and meets with a man outside. The man—balding, with a white, short sleeved buttoned shirt, looks stressed out. After a couple of minutes, Mrs. Simpson steps back on the bus.

"All right, kids. Everybody off and follow me. Leave your bags, we'll be coming back to the bus after the luncheon."

Ten minutes later, we're all sitting at circular tables in a large ballroom on the second floor. White linen covers the tables, and uniformed waiters rush about. This is more formal than I'd expected.

A few minutes later, the boring part begins. A man who looks vaguely familiar takes the podium. I scrunch my eyebrows, trying to place him. Not sure, but I've seen him somewhere at another diplomatic function. Russia? Possibly. That was a long time ago, and I was still pretty young. He introduces himself, but his name isn't at all familiar. In any event, he's from the U.S. Consulate. His presentation is predictably boring, and like a lot of diplomats, a tremendous number of words leave his mouth, almost all of them canceling out the other things he's said, until the end arrives and there's no meaning left at all.

The truth is, I don't listen at all. Instead, my mind keeps returning to Dylan. The look on his face when he closed his eyes. I don't think he knew he has a slight smile on his face, a look of near ecstasy as he sang. Dylan will never be a hard core musician, but what he lacks in talent and experience, he more than makes up for in passion.

He wanted her to know
What he couldn't say with words
My heart nearly stopped when he sang those words.
A view from forever.

How am I ever going to survive going home? Saying goodbye? I love him.

After that thought, I sit up, suddenly interested. The speaker from the US consulate is introducing the

Deputy Chief of Mission from the British Consulate, a woman named Wendy Li. A petite woman, obviously ethnic Chinese, but I've seen her. I'm certain of it. But *where?* Almost certainly in China, but I wasn't sure.

Li begins to speak about the challenges of diplomacy in a country with the conflicts and tensions Israel deals with. She's got a much more engaging presence than whatever-his-name-was, and instead of standing behind the lectern, she walks in front of it and moves around as she speaks, arresting everyone's attention.

I lean close to Dylan and whisper, "I know her. But I don't know where from."

He whispers back, "Not a clue."

"I didn't think you'd have one."

Li continues to talk, then says, "Now, earlier in my career, my first overseas assignment was in Beijing. And while we weren't dealing with the same kind of conflict as here, there were plenty of tensions. In particular, we were preparing to turn Hong Kong back over to China after many years, all at a time when tensions between the United States and China were very high due to spying activities...."

I tilt my head, then lean back to Dylan again. "That's it. I met her in China. Has to be."

"Weren't you a little kid then?"

"I was eight when we moved back to the United States."

Li must have heard something, even as she spoke, because her eyes move to me and stay on me for an uncomfortable minute. She then continues to speak.

I stay quiet for the rest of the presentation, and the question and answer period. Once that's complete, Mrs. Simpson stands up and says, "We'll meet back at the bus in ten minutes, everyone."

I can tell Dylan wants to run for the door so he can grab a cigarette before we all board the bus. No dice. I grab his hand as I stand, because Li is approaching me, a curious—and guarded—expression on her face.

"Excuse me," she says. "I couldn't help but notice you…. is your mother Adelina Thompson?"

Shock hits me. If anyone was going to ask about me, I would have thought they'd ask about my dad.

I nod. "I am… my name's Alexandra."

Li smiles. "Oh, yes. I don't know if you remember me, I'm Wendy Li. You attended the Easter egg hunt at the British embassy in … was it 98? And you fell and hurt your knee."

"Oh my God," I say. "Yes! I knew I remembered you from somewhere. I was seven when that happened."

"You've grown up to be a very beautiful young woman. In fact, you look very like your mother."

That's… an odd compliment.

"How is she?" Li continues.

I open my mouth to speak. Then I close it. I don't have a good answer for that. How is she ever? She's neurotic and has random rages and when she isn't harassing me and the other girls, she's hiding in her room. The only time she's ever happy is when my father is traveling.

Which has been a lot this year.

Li's face softens. With some kind of understanding. She says, "Would you be so kind as to relay a message to her when you see or speak with her?"

I blink. This is bizarre. "Of course," I say.

Li nods, then says, "Please tell her..." She swallows, as if hesitating. Then says, "Please let her know her old friend Kent still wonders how she is doing."

"I've never heard of any friend named Kent," I say.

She shrugs. "Your mother will know. And it's a message she'll appreciate. I promise you. It was a pleasure to meet you, Alexandra. Perhaps we'll meet again some day."

The woman turns and walks away. Dylan asks, "What was that all about?"

I shake my head. "Not a clue. That was ... weird."

"Will you tell your mom?"

I nod. "Yes. Of course. I don't know what to make of it. And I doubt she'll tell me."

Mrs. Simpson pokes her head in the doorway. That's when I realize we're the only people left in the ballroom. "Dylan and Alex. You two... come, please. No hiding out and kissing, we have a schedule."

Chapter Fourteen

Goliath (Dylan)

AFTER WE LEAVE the embassy, the next stop is the high school. It's an older school, built of the same tan stone as every other building in Jerusalem, and like the rest of the city, it has a radically different feel than Haifa and Tel Aviv. As if it's been ripped out of the past. Even the students here are dressed more conservatively.

Well, not all of them. Mrs. Simpson and the principal of the school conduct a small assembly, where we are introduced to our host students.

I size up my host student as we approach each other to shake hands.

"Amir," he says.

"Dylan."

We shake hands. Amir wears blue jeans, a pair of Converse shoes with the Grinch on the sides, a Morbid Obesity t-shirt and has a necklace with a golden Mickey Mouse pendant. My first impression: a hipster with lousy taste in music.

"You have everything?" he asks, eyeing my one bag and guitar case.

"I do," I say.

"Come!" The students are dispersing. That's quick.

"Hold on," I say. "I need to say goodbye to someone."

I turn, looking for Alex. She's standing thirty feet away, talking with a girl who is far less trendy than Amir, which is probably a good thing. "Alex!" I call.

Alex raising a finger, as if to say, "One minute," then she turns to me.

"I'll see you later?"

She smiles, then leads forward and gives me a kiss on the cheek.

Then I'm headed off with Amir to God knows where.

It turns out it's not far at all—we don't ride or take the bus, but rather walk the three blocks from the high school. Amir lives in a narrow townhouse in a row of identical townhouses, all of them made with the same blocks of stone as every other building I've seen. On the doorpost is a narrow rectangular case, maybe six inches long, with brightly-colored and elaborate decorations. Amir touches the doorpost in an obviously-reverent way as we enter the apartment. I make a note to ask Amir about it later. For now, I follow him through the door. I'm promptly swamped with introductions to his parents, Aaron and Hannah, and his four younger brothers and sisters, whose names I don't catch. The rest of the night we spend talking. I learn that the box on the door is a *mezuzah*, and there's one on every door in the house, and they have something to do with prayers or scriptures which are handwritten and placed inside the box. Amir's family is not Hasidic, but they are very conservative Orthodox Jews.

Then I get a stunning and pleasant surprise. Despite their surplus of children, Aaron has arranged for me to have *my own room* during my stay here. It's the size of a closet, but it only has one bed in it. Apparently it belongs to Brad, the youngest of the children, who has been bumped to a pallet on the floor in one of the other bedrooms. I have to share the room with kids toys, including an appallingly large Barney the Dinosaur, but I can live with that, because I don't have to share the room with someone who snores, masturbates, or otherwise makes my life miserable.

The next morning it's raining and *cold*. I didn't think it got cold in the Middle East. But when I step on the back balcony to have a cigarette with a cup of coffee, I find myself shivering.

Amir follows me out onto the back porch.

"My parents won't speak anything, but they don't approve of smoke."

"My mother doesn't either," I say.

He chuckles. "You like Jerusalem?"

I shrug. "I haven't seen enough of it yet. Though I'm fascinated by the Old City. I'd love to go there."

His face looks clouded. Then he says, "We don't go there any more."

"No?" I asked. Inside, I felt a hit of disappointment. Selfish, I suppose, but real.

He shakes his head. "My father was injured at the Western Wall two years ago while praying. A riot started—he was hit in the head with a thrown rock. We haven't been back since."

"I'm sorry."

He shrugs. "It's the Arabs. They know nothing but violence. In their own countries, they cut off the hands of thieves and behead adulterers. Here they kill our people."

I don't answer, because I don't have an answer. All I've heard here, over and over again, is how awful the Arabs are. But then I think about going to the *Arab* school in Haifa, where they get a separate and not-so-equal education. And my mind runs over the body count Wendy Li mentioned yesterday. 660 Palestinians killed in Israeli attacks the same year 23 Israelis were killed by Palestinians. I don't have any answers, and I don't know who is right or wrong, and I don't really know the history. But I can see the difference between a David and Goliath.

Still, almost everyone I'd met had been touched in one way or another by the conflict. Yossi's father killed. Amir's father injured in a riot. People here were terrified, and people who are scared will do crazy stuff.

I sigh. I'd lay money that more people were killed in just the city of New York last year. I need to check on that.

"What time do you head to school?" I ask.

"In about half an hour," he says. "Do you know your schedule today?"

I shake my head. "I think we're supposed to split up into groups and speak at a couple of different schools. But I'm not sure where."

It turns out that we do, in fact, split up. The bad news? The girls all go to a girl's school halfway across town, while we speak at a *yeshiva* in the German colony. Except for a few minutes early in the morning, I don't see Alex all day.

I miss her. With our time so short—only eight days left—every minute without her is agony. So even though our visit to the *Yeshiva* is interesting, I'm anxious to get back to Alex the entire time. Normally I would find it fascinating. It has a mixed curriculum, primarily study of the Torah and other Jewish scriptures, but with some component of secular subjects including math, languages, and science. I'm surprised to learn that many *yeshivas* have no secular teaching at all—the students *only* study scripture. I suppose they wouldn't have had a bunch of American high school students come speak at one of those, however. Here, the students sit in pairs at large tables in a huge classroom, books spread out before them. The boys all wear identical clothes: black pants and shoes, white button down shirts. Many of the boys have sidecurls instead of trimmed sideburns. John asks about it during the assembly—it turns out there is a Biblical injunction against cutting the hair in front of the ears, or sometimes beards, and it's all very confusing.

We take a tour through the *yeshiva* itself after the assembly. Though the boys study weighty stuff during the day, the school seems to have a lot of normal (and not so normal) amenities: weight rooms, a gym, basketball courts and extremely crowded dormitories. After the tour, we eat lunch—no different than any other lunch we've eaten in Israel—then give presentations to another group of students. It's early afternoon before we leave.

We meet back up with our host students at the high school a little before three in the afternoon. As soon as Alex and I see each other, she runs over and throws her arms around me.

She whispers, "I missed you."

"I missed you," I say.

"A bunch of the host students are gathering tonight somewhere. You joining?"

"Yeah, if I can."

The touch of her body against mine is electrifying. I slide my fingertips down her back, brushing the muscles along her spine. She's beautiful, and brilliant, but part of what I love about her is her inner strength. Holding her in my arms now, all of my attention is focused on her, shutting out the rest of the world.

So both of us are a little startled at the sound of someone clearing their throat next to us. We separate, and suddenly I feel awkward, a little embarrassed.

"I'm Rebekah," says the girl who interrupted us, smiling at me. "Alex's host."

"Dylan," I respond.

"Alex, I'm sorry, my parents are here already. We have to go."

Alex nods. Then she looks back at me, her green eyes flashing. She takes one of my hands. "If I don't see you later... maybe you can call?"

"I'll try," I say. I don't want to let go.

"But try to come. We're meeting at some cafe on Ben Yehuda."

"I'll try," I repeat. Then I pull her to me, putting my hands on her waist and looking her in the eye. "If I don't see you, I'll dream about you."

She blinks, as if startled by the words, then stands on her tiptoes and kisses me. A moment later, she's gone.

Nickel Mines (Alex)

I've lived in several countries, and I know better than to make broad assumptions about any place I go to. People are people everywhere—they have different tastes, ideas, activities, beliefs. But all the same, I'm surprised when Rebekah and I arrive on the bus at Ben Yehuda street in the heart of West Jerusalem.

The streets are tan cobblestones, polished by decades of pedestrians walking on the stones, and the entire street is blocked to vehicles. On either side of the street are three-story buildings, with hundreds of people walking, standing, shopping and otherwise occupying themselves.

The next thing I notice is loud dance music pouring out of the open doors of a club. A queue winds around the block. Teenagers and college-age kids are in the line (mostly), all of them very carefully dressed to appear that they dressed casually. Lots of loosely-fit tank tops, and lots of bell bottoms, even though those vanished from the American scene a year or more ago. Across the street from the club, two restaurants, side by side, have tables spilling out into the street. A small band, including a drummer, are set up in the street with guitar cases open to collect cash as they play. Hundreds of people stand around, talking and laughing. Almost everywhere else in Jerusalem, you see people of varying ages, in a variety of costumes—casual clothing, business, military uniforms, the long black coats of Hasidic Jews and the *kuffeeyah* of Arab men. But here, the dress is almost universally young, casual, and secular.

Rebekah leads the way, clearly knowing exactly where she is headed. I follow closely, because if I lose her in this crowd, I'll be lost forever. I haven't heard from Dylan this afternoon, and I don't have his host student's phone number, so I have no idea if he's coming tonight. I hope so. We barely saw each other today and that's not fair.

I spot Dylan and his host student just a moment later. Dylan has a stern expression on his face, his eyebrows drawn closely together. He's following along behind his host student—Amir, I think his name is—and neither of them look happy. A peculiar tension ripples between them.

Dylan's shoulders drop a full inch when he sees me and he lets out a long breath. I've never seen him look so relieved. He moves toward me quickly, abandoning Amir. I lift my face toward his and we're in each other's arms, his lips are on mine and everything is exactly the way it should be. His hands slip up almost to my shoulders and I rest my face against his chest.

I open my mouth, say "I—" and close it suddenly. I almost said *I love you*. My heart is racing, my pulse loud in my ears. I haven't said those words—neither has he. We've only got a few days left. What happens if we *never* say it? What happens if we go home and I never tell him how I feel?

Does he even feel that way about me? We haven't talked about it. We both said this was temporary, that we're just having fun, that we're just going to see what happens while we're on this trip. But it's not temporary, is it? Not the way I feel. Not if he goes home and we never say it. Not if we go back to the United States and *never see each other again.* Maybe our relationship on this trip is temporary. But there's no way this cavern of pain in my chest at the thought of losing him could be temporary.

"Maybe you two should get a room." The sarcastic words jerk me back to the present. It's Elle, wearing a skirt which is shorter than is probably legal in Jerusalem. She's standing next to an obviously uncomfortable girl with long chestnut hair. I slowly become aware that my host student, and Dylan's, look equally uncomfortable.

Dylan just smiles at Elle and murmurs in his smooth southern accent, "Maybe we should."

Heat flashes up my face. But I keep a grip on his hand.

We all set off as a group, going further down the street. A few moments later we run into John and Mike with their hosts, and Megan not long after. Dylan is curiously quiet as we walk, his eyes darting everywhere and taking in our surroundings. The rest of our group is loud, chatty, and excited, so Dylan and I find ourselves trailing a little bit behind, just walking and holding hands.

"I love it here," he says. His voice is very quiet as he says the words. "There's something just magical about this place."

He must be tired. Whenever he's sleepy his Southern accent is thicker, and the way he said "*jes magical*" was dripping with mint juleps and kudzu. I squeeze his hand.

Our host students lead the way through the crowds, which grow thicker as we move further down the street. We pass a street band, acoustic guitar and drums and a ragged-looking girl with stringy red hair, singing in a wailing, tinny voice. We finally stop at a cafe, where everyone gathers around two tables they push together on the sidewalk.

An officious waiter, obviously displeased to be serving a group of teenagers, distributes menus and glasses of water. Dylan leans close to me and we look over the menu together. "That looks really good," I say, pointing to a delicious-looking lemon raspberry dacquoise.

"What is it?" he asks.

"It's um… meringue… whipped cream… trust me, it's delicious."

"I'm not all that hungry," he says, his eyes dropping to the table. "But you go ahead."

A couple minutes later the waiter reappears and we begin to order. I get the dessert—I'll get Dylan to share with me, hopefully—and coffee. Dylan just asks for water.

After the waiter is gone, I lean close to Dylan and whisper, "Is everything okay?"

"Yeah," he replies, "Why?" His voice sounds unnatural as he says the words.

"You just seem weird."

"I'm fine."

"All right." I don't really mean it. When Dylan says, "I'm fine," that usually means something's wrong but he doesn't want to talk about it. We've only known each other a few weeks, but that's been long enough to learn that about him. But I also know pushing probably won't help. So I shift my attention to the conversation across the table, between Dylan's host student—I think his name his Amir—and John.

Oh...

I feel immediately uncomfortable when I realize the topic. *Morbid Obesity's* new album, which went platinum the day it came out. The title song *Nickel Mines* has been crazy controversial—it's about the murder of several girls at an Amish school in Nickel Mines, Pennsylvania last year.

Amir is waving his hands, a passionate expression on his face as he talks about it. "It's brilliant. The song completely subverts everything you'd expect."

I swallow. I don't want to talk about this, I want to change the subject. It happens sometimes at home of course—but everyone knows Crank is my brother-in-law. No one here knows, because I haven't talked about it.

Dylan shakes his head. "I don't buy it. They're looking for attention. Making money off someone else's tragedy."

That's like a punch in the gut. I shake my head. "No. It's not."

"Come on, Alex. The girls in that school were all murdered. Crank Wilson was looking for controversy to drum up sales, and he got it. He's using them."

I shake my head again. "That's not true." I feel like my tongue is lead. I remember when Julia talked about the song last Christmas. Crank and Julia had just finished writing it two days before. She had tears in her eyes as she talked about it. Julia can't have children, and more and more lately I think she's coming to feel that as an intense loss.

Somehow I didn't want to say all that. Sometimes people at school want to be my friend just because of Julia and Crank. They're big stars, and the other kids think they can use me to get tickets or backstage passes or invitations to dinner. It's infuriating, and it's disheartening too. I want to be liked for *me*. I didn't want anyone on this trip to know about them, because that would start off all the same old questions. *What's it like having a rock star in the family? Isn't Crank hot? Is it true Crank and Serena are having an affair?*

Instead of saying any of that, I just stumble over my words. "They wouldn't do that."

Dylan looks angry, his eyebrows drawn together. "Of course they would! That's what I hate about people sometimes. Rich people using poor people. Do you have *any* idea what it's like to be living on the street? I guarantee you Crank Wilson never saw what the streets looked like." The others at the table quiet down. I think they just realized this discussion is getting serious.

"You have no idea what you're talking about." The words come out in a sharper tone than I'd intended.

His nostrils flare. He's really angry. "I know *exactly* what I'm talking about Alex. I'm not the one going home to a millionaire family where everything gets handed to me."

His words make me want to cry. In a strangled sort of voice I say, "Why are you being such a dick?"

Somewhere in the background I hear someone groan.

"Because I don't like it when people who have everything use people who have nothing!"

"Well I don't like it when people are being self-righteous *assholes*!" I stand up and look at Rebekah. She moves almost immediately to her feet. "Can we go?" I ask, fighting back angry tears.

I don't wait for an answer, turning to walk away. Only then does Dylan change his awful tone of voice. He calls out my name, panicky. "Alex—"

"Leave me alone," I say. Then I finally make it away, out into the crowd, where he can't see me cry.

CHAPTER FIFTEEN

Stupid (Dylan)

WHY ARE YOU being such a dick?

Leave me alone.

Her words have been echoing in my stupid empty head all night, bouncing off the perfectly smooth inner lining of my skull and all the empty space in between.

I don't know why she was so upset about it. People have opinions all the time. She and I have differing opinions about a lot of things, including plenty of pop culture things. But clearly *this* is somehow personal to her. And that was perfectly clear well before I'd gone off the rails.

Stupid.

I ache inside in a way I'd never experienced before. I'd been lonely. I've had girlfriends, and I've had break-ups before. But this… it's different. I feel… empty. Like someone punched a hole through my chest. I barely spoke last night as Amir and I returned to his apartment, me shambling along like a *stupid* zombie, and I … it makes me realize that this has gotten far more serious than I realized.

I love her. There's no question.

And I'm scared. Because I have to go home, and I don't know if I'll ever see her again.

At 3 o'clock in the morning I stumble out of the room and down the hall and I turn on the computer in the living room. I haven't been online since that asshole told me Spot was dead. I find myself gritting my teeth, my face twisting up in knots as I try to hold back any possibility of tears.

When the computer boots up, I log into Facebook. No messages, but Alex had posted a series of pictures of us both. Arm in arm, holding each other with the backdrop of the Sea of Galilee behind us. Laughing together at the market in Nazareth. Embracing, our foreheads touching, a faint smile on her face, just a couple of days ago.

Her status message a couple of days ago: *Dylan Paris wrote a song for me.*

I have to make it up to her somehow. But I don't even know why she's so upset. I Google *Morbid Obesity Nickel Mines*—maybe it's something about the song?

The answer shouts out to me almost immediately. Crank Wilson did an interview with *FHM* when the movie came out. There's a photograph of him in the online version holding a beautiful woman with curly brown hair and green eyes that match Alex's. She looks a lot like Alex.

The article identifies her as Crank's wife Julia—the daughter of former US Ambassador Richard Thompson.

Holy. Shit.

Crank is Alex's brother-in-law?

I read through the article and it all begins to make sense.

In explaining the genesis of *Nickel Mines*, Wilson was quick to explain that the significance of the song was deeply personal. "This summer Julia and I found out she can't have children. And the idea that someone would murder children—both of us broke down a little when we heard about it. And the really just incredible part—what inspired me to write the song—was how the Amish community—the families of those girls—were so quick to forgive. They reached out to the family of the killer. It was shocking and somehow humbling, because most people would have been screaming for revenge."

I'm stunned. I continue reading through and unfortunately learn a little about Crank's background. He wasn't what I thought he was. His Dad was a cop, and he left home when he was sixteen. Brother with autism. Mother had left home after some kind of hospitalization.

In short, I'd been a judgmental asshole.

The really frustrating thing is that I'm not going to see her today—for the second day in a row, the group is splitting up and going to different schools to speak. Alex and I got assigned to different groups for this one. I don't know if we'll get a chance to talk, but I can at least leave her a note. I search online and find an image of a cat—Alex loves cats, God only knows why—with a caption which reads "I'm sorry." I copy the image and post it to her Facebook wall, then go to bed. This time I quickly fall asleep.

It wasn't in Atlanta (Alex)

My first reaction this morning, when I see the picture of the kitten in a paper bag with the caption "I'm sorry!!!" is mild annoyance. *Oh, that's original.* But then I think it through. Dylan doesn't own a computer. Until we met he didn't have a Facebook account. So this actually is original in a way.

And the kitten is cute.

He was still being an asshole. It's one thing to have an opinion—even if it is misinformed, ignorant. But it's another thing entirely to turn on me.

I know exactly *what I'm talking about Alex. I'm not the one going home to a millionaire family where everything gets handed to me.*

That, of course, zeroed in on one of the biggest differences between us. I casually spend money—my parents sent me with a thousand dollars in cash, plus a credit card in the event of an emergency. I'm pretty sure Dylan came on this trip with less than two hundred dollars in his pocket. So all along, he's been super careful what he bought (except for cigarettes) while I've spent freely. It's meant he had to turn down opportunities to go out with everyone, or he orders the barest minimum, saying *I'm not hungry* when it's obvious that's not true. But he won't let me buy anything for him.

So I get it. He's really uncomfortable about money. He threw that barb at me. He lashed out at *Crank* of all people. Crank and Julia might be doing pretty well now, but he's from as working class a background as it gets.

More than that, they'd worked incredibly hard to be where they are. And even more than that...

I'm going in circles. I flop back on the bed and open my email.

A message from Julia.

Dear Alexandra,

I got a call from the investigator we hired in Atlanta. He normally handles divorces and corporate stuff, but said he found this interesting.

The short version: we don't have any results. He's searched the records for deaths in Atlanta in the last two years, then focused in on homeless teenage girls. If she died, it wasn't in Atlanta. He gave all kinds of limitations—like if she was in a distant suburb. Right now we don't know much of anything.

The next step will be going beyond records searches—he can go question people, talk to people who are homeless, ask around. That might turn up more information. And it might not. No guarantees. It's hard to find someone when you don't know their name.

Let me know what you want to do. Money isn't an issue here.

I hope your trip is going well and that Dylan is turning out to be everything you wanted.

I love you,
Julia

I don't hesitate. I hit reply and rapidly type: *Please keep looking. Love, Alex.*

There. I did it.

Now I just need to see Dylan again.

Except I don't (Dylan)

"Amir, listen, I need to go see Alex. Do you know where her — what's her host student's name? Rebekah?"

"She just lives a couple of blocks away, but you can't just—"

"I can. I have to see her."

It's already getting dark—nightfall has been coming earlier and earlier. And it's chilly outside, more than it has been this entire trip, and more than I expected it to ever be. I always pictured the Middle East as just heat and sand. Amir doesn't look happy.

"I have homework to do. But I can walk you over there. You'll have to find your way back."

"Great!" I say.

I throw on a sweatshirt, which I need because my jacket is really too light for the temperature outside. Who knew? Five minutes later I'm walking beside Amir on the Jerusalem sidewalk. Heavy traffic goes by us, commuters on their way home from work, headlights on, brains turned off, horns honking and tires occasionally screeching. It looks frustrating, really. I'm glad I'm on foot.

We turn down a side street, then Amir points out the door. I trot up the three steps to a large townhouse constructed of the same tan stone as everything else in the city. One thing Jerusalem has no shortage of is rocks.

I knock on the door. Suddenly anxious, I slide my hands into my jacket pockets. What if she won't forgive me? I was kind of an asshole, and that's not even considering that it was her family I was talking about. She's got every right to be mad. And we've never had a fight before. I don't know what she's like in a fight. Is she vengeful? Is she going to write me off? This is agonizing. Especially because we've hardly got any time left at all. I don't want to waste it fighting.

I didn't mean to snap at her with that comment about not going home to a millionaire family. We've talked enough about her home life that I know it's no picnic. Her father's always gone and her mother's crazy. At least my mom got it together and has been there for me. *Really* been there for me, even when it was incredibly tough on her.

A man opens the door. He's in his early forties, I think, and wearing an army uniform, the sleeves rolled up revealing powerful arms. His black, tightly curled hair is cut short, and he looks like he needs to shave.

He looks at me with a sour face, then says something in Hebrew.

I shuffle on my feet a little bit, cough, then say, "I don't speak Hebrew... I was looking for Alex?"

The soldier rolls his eyes. Then he turns away and closes the door in my face. I'm left standing on the steps, wondering if he's just gone away for good, or is he going to go get her, or do I have the wrong house?

A long minute later the door yanks open again. It's her.

"Dylan," she says.

"Alex... um... can we talk a minute?"

She nods, but doesn't say any words.

I step back, forgetting I'm standing on the top of a set of stairs. For just a second I feel that sickening empty feeling—you know the one, when you put your foot down and *there's nothing there*—then I begin to fall backwards. I try to put my foot behind me, my stomach suddenly twisting, and throw my foot back trying to catch something while my arms do a crazy windmill motion as I lose my balance and stumble back down the three stairs to the sidewalk.

I twist and land—somehow—almost on my knees, crouched way down.

"Well, that was... dignified..." I say.

Alex giggles. But she stays standing at the top of the stairs.

I stand up, feeling myself flush. I have to crane my neck to face her.. "I—Alex..."

She arches one eyebrow. What does that mean?

I falter for a second, then I start to speak again. "Alex... listen... I'm sorry about yesterday."

Her eyes water just slightly, but she blinks them, forces it back. Then she says, "Why did you say it?"

"About Crank? I ... I just didn't know. I didn't know about his past, I didn't know he was family to you."

"Would it have made a difference?" A furrow appears between her eyebrows as she asks the question.

I nod. "Yeah. I mean... I just... I made assumptions... I was wrong."

She sighs. "What about me?"

I swallow and look down. "Alex, I'm sorry. It just—look—I was an asshole."

"Why?" she cries out.

Because I'm afraid. Because I love you. Because I'm afraid of losing you. Because I'm an idiot. I swallow, then choke out, "Saying goodbye to you is going to hurt worse than anything. Ever."

Tears roll down her face. She moves down the steps—much more gracefully than I had—then comes close. She puts a hand on my face and whispers, "Me too."

I open my mouth. *I love you*, I say. Except I don't. My terrified throat closes on the words and snuffs them out.

CHAPTER SIXTEEN

You look acceptable (Dylan)

WAKE UP ON the morning of December 6 with a deep sense of dread. Today is our last full day in Jerusalem—tomorrow we'll be bussing back to Tel Aviv for two days of wrap up meetings and I don't know what all. Then we fly back to the United States.

Amir wants to talk this morning, but I'm just not in a space to do it. I want to be a better guest, and be friendly and witty and diplomatic. Instead, I sit out on the porch silently drinking my coffee and smoking a cigarette. Eventually he gives up trying to talk and just sits down.

After a few minutes he tries one more time. "What's gotten into you, Dylan?"

I sigh. "Going home," I say.

He grunts knowingly. "You don't live near Alex, do you?"

I grunt. Then I say, "Take your entire country. Turn it lengthwise, then lay it out from end to end. Do that ten times over. That's how far."

He nods. Then he says, "My older brother had a long distance relationship like that. Really long distance."

"Oh yeah?"

He nods. "They met when we were vacationing in Greece. She's from Paris."

"Oh. Yeah, that's a long way." Longer, probably, than it is from Atlanta to San Francisco. "What happened?"

"He ended up going to college in Paris. He proposed to her in the Louvre—they've been married five years now."

I feel a smile growing on my face. I can't imagine any sort of dramatic proposal scene—that's not my style. But on some level, the thought of proposing to Alex makes me very happy.

Idiot. You haven't even told her you love her.

"Thanks, Amir. That's good to hear."

A few minutes later we're gathering our things to leave. Usually when we're going to be on tour buses all day I'll take my guitar along, but today the group is only going a short distance. We'll be touring the Old City on foot, so they advised us to dress warm and not carry much.

Amir and I walk to the high school. As we walk he treats me to a monologue of the state of the Israeli music scene. He goes on about punk and semi-punk bands who are all heavily influenced by the Clash, the B52s, Dirty Rotten Imbeciles, Morbid Obesity, Mooke, Shabek Samech. I've never heard of any of them except the Clash and Morbid Obesity. Amir feels very strongly about Morbid Obesity, and tells me that I'd made a tremendous mistake the other night.

"Really, Dylan, if I had been your girlfriend when you said that stuff, I wouldn't have taken you back."

I chuckle a little. A moment later we arrive at the high school. Amir waves and heads off to class—I join the small group of Americans in the courtyard.

Alex is already here—she sees me and smiles, then walks over and wraps her arms around me, leaning her forehead against my chest.

I take a deep, longing breath. She feels so warm. I close my eyes, breathing in the scent of strawberry from her hair and lilies from her perfume. Every time we kiss I die a little. What will I do without her? Over the last few days, my focus has narrowed in on that upcoming separation. With that thought, I grip her even tighter, my arms around her waist.

She moves with the same instinct, her arms over my shoulders. She leans her head back, her eyes half closed. I can feel her breath, hot against my skin. I lean forward and our lips touch. Her mouth opens, ours tongues touching greedily, and I suck at her lip. She gives a soft moan.

"You guys should get a room," Mike says as he walks by. He claps me on the shoulder, harder than is necessary.

It's enough to pull me back to the surface. I pull back from Alex just enough to look in her green eyes, searching the depths of them as if might find answers to life's questions in her.

"You look beautiful this morning," I say. The words come out rough.

Her cheeks flash bright red. But she isn't really fazed. In a nonchalant tone, she says, "You look acceptable."

I grin. "I'm relieved to hear you think so."

She grabs the sides of my face and aggressively plans a kiss right on my face. Then she steps back.

The sudden distance between us is jarring, but tempered by the fact that she immediately grips one of my hands. We turn and walk together toward the rest of the group.

"Dylan and Alex, I'm so glad the two of you could join us." I can't tell if Mrs. Simpson is being sarcastic or not. Her attitude toward me and Alex has become more tolerant in the last few days—I suspect because she won't have to put up with us much longer. But moments later she gets down to business. A guide from the tourist bureau or something like that is going to be here in a moment and will walk us over to the Old City. From there, we'll be on a guided tour.

She lays down the rules. No wandering off alone. We'll be allowed to shop or get something in the area overlooking the Western Wall during lunchtime. Otherwise, we have to stay with the group at all times. If we're approached by shopkeepers ("and you will be," interjects the guy from the tourist bureau) then simply say no-thank you and keep going.

When she wraps up, he says, "Before we go, I must make a few more comments. It's unlikely that anything should happen while you are in the city. But if it does— if there is any kind of altercation or violence—stay together as a group and seek the assistance of the nearest policeman or soldier. *Do not* go on your own."

Alex looks troubled, as do many of the students. "Is it that dangerous?" I ask.

He shakes his head. "Statistically, it's probably far safer than cities in America. But the streets of Jerusalem were laid out three thousand years ago. It's extremely easy for you to get lost. Should that happen, you must ask for assistance getting back to the plaza in front of the Western Wall. That is where we shall meet."

Five minutes later we move out as a group. Alex and I trail along behind the rest of the group—not far behind, but in the back of the crowd—holding hands and walking together. It's only a few blocks from the school to Jaffa Gate. But before we reach the gate, we're walking down a long, long sidewalk, the high walls of the city towering over us. Tan stone, fifty feet high and topped with battlements, the outer wall of the Old City is fascinating. I've never travelled anywhere before, and this place is utterly alien, but also incredibly fascinating. Alex seems to be feeling some of the same emotions, the grip of her hands growing stronger. We're moving faster now, trying to hear the guide from the tourist bureau as he begins to detail the history of the walls—some of which have been standing here since Jesus's time or earlier.

And then we are there, walking through the massive gate with its pointed stone arches. Around us, a melange of tourists, soldiers, Arabs, Jews, more. Two men in black suits with wide-brimmed black hats, long full beards and locks of hair growing in curls in front of their ears—Hasidic Jews—enter the gates in front of us. Our guide stops and faces us, telling a story about the recapture of the city by Israel during the 1967 war. I've heard a great deal about this particular war since I arrived in Israel—far more than I ever wanted to, to be honest.

Once inside the walls, we're faced with a seemingly-chaotic scene, a broad plaza with dozens of people in every direction. It takes me a few moments to make sense of the scene. On the left are several buildings,with shops, the Tourism Bureau, money changers, and a coffee shop. To the right is a limited amount of parking, no more than a dozen Mercedes Benz taxis backed up against the thousand-year-old-wall. As we move forward, we crowd around the guide. My eyes are on the signs, written in multiple languages. The St. Michel Cafeteria. Versavee Bistro Bar & Cafe. The Franciscan Book Shop. A street sign in three languages points to Greek Catholic Patriarchate Street. The Franciscan Corner (no idea what is inside the building) next to a wide open clothing store next to a shop advertising stamps, film and tattoos. In large black letters, the SWEDISH CHRISTIAN STUDY CENTER is one floor above Petra Souvenirs and Money Changers.

Quickly, though, our guide leads us to a narrow street—by street, I mean an alley, maybe twelve feet wide, moving slightly downhill with occasional steps. No cars move on this street—it's strictly pedestrian only. On both sides, we're crowded by dozens of shops selling everything from tourist goods to brass candlesticks. Men stand inside or just at the front of each shop—the shops are tiny, few of them with even enough space to sit down. Awnings block out most of the sky, and the tourists are *everywhere*. But not just tourists. Soldiers. Children. It's hard to tell whether the tourists are here for the city or if the city is here for the tourists. After all, Jerusalem has been a place of pilgrimage for centuries.

"Keep moving, keep moving," our guide says. It's hard to listen. I'm craning my neck everywhere, and Alex has taken out her camera and is shooting pictures of everything. And seriously, she's lived in China and Russia and God only knows where else. If *she* finds this fascinating and a little magical, then it must really be.

I can hear half a dozen different languages being spoken. The shopkeepers ignore us, seeking fatter prey than me (I'm down to my last $20 and it must show). We keep moving forward, Alex's hand in mine, and I can't imagine a more perfect day.

We reach an intersection—if you could call it that—and our guide stops and turns, beckoning us to gather around him. On either side of the intersection, the street gives up any pretense of viewing the sky—the buildings arch over the street completely. To the right, it's obviously new—polished light-colored stone, well lit, with only a few shops. Ahead, the street continues to descend downhill. To our left, the street is also almost completely covered over by slanted awnings that meet in the center of the street. Dozens of shops, hundreds of colors, chaos leading off into the distance.

The smells are vivid. Some good—floral fragrances pouring out of a clothes store, the crisp frying of falafel at at a stand nearby—some bad—the faintest hint of garbage wafting from somewhere, along with the accumulated body odor of two thousand years of tourists who have made their way through this city.

Most of the shops are tourist goods—"I went to Jerusalem and all I got was this lousy t-shirt", carpets, jewelry, antique pottery. But some are more prosaic—a tiny hardware store, a corner grocery. While this city may be one of the most crowded (and certainly oldest) tourist destinations in the world, it is also home to many of the people around us. Our guide explains to us that the area to the left leads to the Christian and Muslim quarters of the city. To the right is the Jewish quarter. For centuries, different religious and ethnic groups maintained their own sections of the city. We turn left. The streets here are dark, completely covered over after a few feet, and not well-lit, though plenty of light comes from the shops—that is, those that are open. I'm surprised by just how many are shuttered, at least a third of them. Graffiti in Arabic, Hebrew and sometimes English is written on the shutters. A tremendous amount of graffiti on every surface, some of it elaborate and beautiful, much of it ugly.

We're moving very slowly now, our guide leading his way through the crowded market with all of us trailing behind. Mrs. Simpson has moved to the rear, occasionally saying, "Dylan and Alex, keep up with the group," in a surprisingly tolerant tone.

Alex leans close to me and squeezes my hand tight and whispers, "I wish this day could last forever."

Via Dolorosa (Alex)

Even though I've lived in a lot of places, I don't think I've ever been in any city quite so magical as the Old City of Jerusalem. The sights and sounds are astonishing. From everywhere, the smells of spices, the shouts of the shopkeepers, the cacophony of colors. But above all, it's discovering the city with Dylan that makes it so wonderful

As we tour the city, we spend an hour at the Church of the Holy Sepulcher, an ancient building which is controlled by a dozen different denominations of Christianity. I buy a rosary for my mother.

Outside, we are allowed to spend one hour in a very limited part of the market. Our boundaries are one street, no further than the corners. This particular street is wider than most of the others, with plenty of sunlight. Two coffee shops and a restaurant are on this street along with the expected tourist traps. At one of the shops, Dylan insists on buying us matching coffee mugs, digitally printed on the spot with a picture of the two of us.

From there we move on to the plaza in front of the western wall. The wall, once the retaining wall of one side of a Jewish temple which was destroyed 2000 years ago, is now a holy place where devout Jews come from all over the world to pray. I read that this plaza used to be known as the Moroccan quarter, but that it was leveled three days after the 1967 war ended. The residents were evicted, and the entire area was turned into a giant plaza. At the same time our tour guide tells us that the reason the Jewish quarter looks so new is that the Jordanians leveled that part of the city during the 1948 war. The competing claims and the constant justification that we hear at every stop are making me increasingly cynical about both sides of the conflict. Dylan meanwhile, has seemed almost disturbed. He's increasingly sympathetic to the Palestinians, and I think that bothers him.

At the plaza, we stop to have lunch. We have an hour here, so each of us has the opportunity to approach the wall. Dylan and I go together. And while I don't pray very often, I do find myself giving a short prayer when I'm standing at the wall. I pray for peace. And selfishly, I pray that Dylan and I will have a chance for a future.

As we walk away from the wall, I try to imagine that future and I shiver. He wants to go travel after high school for a year or more. After that, he doesn't really have plans. That's inconceivable to me. All I *have* is plans, whether I like them or not.

Dylan feels me shiver. I think he mistakes it, thinking it's because of the cool breeze coming across the plaza, because he pulls me close, wrapping an arm around my waist. I lean my head on his shoulder.

"I'm gonna miss this place," he says.

"I will too," I reply. I'm going to miss *you*. I don't know why he doesn't say that. I don't even know why I don't say it.

The tour continues through the afternoon, away from the Western Wall toward Damascus Gate and the market there, then back to the Via Dolorosa, the road that Jesus took through the city on the way to his crucifixion. It's getting late, and there are fewer people on the streets. I'm silent as we follow the steps up that narrow road, passing apartments and hostels, pottery and antique stores, gaudy tourist shops. We stop to look at an inscription in Latin, marking one of the stations of the Cross. I can only imagine what my mother, a devout Catholic, would have given to be here right now.

For me, as we wind up the narrow street, I feel a shadow coming over me. With the clattering sound of metal on metal, shopkeepers behind and ahead of us roll down shutters, closing business for the day. It's late in the afternoon and their departure gives the city a for-lorn, abandoned air.

Suddenly I realize that this is it. We won't have an-other opportunity to be here in the Old City, and in the morning we go back to Tel Aviv. My eyes start to water, and I blink them frantically before Dylan sees.

But he does see. He leans close and whispers, "Me too."

I wave down Mrs. Simpson, following behind at the back of the group, and ask her to take a picture of us to-gether. I think she senses our sadness, because she takes the picture without comment.

You'll find a way (Dylan)

The streets are almost empty as Amir and I make our way to the high school. It's Friday; the sabbath starts at sundown, and today is also the first Friday in Ha-nukah. Amir has explained to me that Hanukah isn't anything like the biggest of the Jewish Holidays, but I always think of it that way because of its proximity to Christmas.

As we trudge along, he says, "You fly out tomorrow?"

"Sunday," I say.

"Oh, right," he replies. Tomorrow we have a lunch with our hosts from all three cities, along with Americans in the other two groups. That's to be followed by a party (more like a wake), and then we fly out the next morning.

I've been feeling glum ever since we left the Old City. I finally got around to posting a status update on Facebook for the first time last night. It simply said, "Bummer to be leaving."

Alex had posted the picture of the two of us on the Via Dolorosa. Her eyes were watery in the picture, a little red. I maintained a pokerface. I don't know why, except that it's just what I do. I wish I could go back in time thirty days and live this last month over again, and over, and over even one more time. I wish I could hold her in my arms always.

The bus, yet another tour bus, is parked in front of the school, and the driver is already loading people's bags. I set my guitar case and backpack down and just stand there. Alex isn't here yet.

"You take good care of yourself," Amir says. "And tell Alex I wish her to be well."

"I will."

Awkwardly, he sticks out a hand to shake. I take it, and we shake hands, and then he's gone.

A few moments later, a white station wagon which looks like it's from the nineties stops at the curb and Alex gets out, along with her host family. They fuss over her, helping her get her bags to the bus. The mother is red-eyed and Rebekah is weeping and she and Alex hug for a long time. Then they step back, as Mrs. Simpson gives the word to get on the bus, and we all begin to pile on. I walk over and take Alex's hand.

Rebekah, who I barely know, runs over and hugs Alex one more time. Then she wraps her arms around me and squeezes, and whispers in my ear, "Take care of her."

Confused, I reply, "We're going home to different places."

She shakes her head and squeezes a little tighter. "You'll find a way if it matters to you." Then she lets go and steps back.

The words spear through me. I sag a little. Then I take Alex's hand again, and we get on the bus.

It takes almost ten more minutes before everyone is seated. We're quiet, sitting in our seat, holding hands. Alex leans against me. Finally, everyone is on board. Mrs. Simpson stands up and does a head count. Everyone's here.

She nods to the bus driver, who closes the door. He starts the engine, a whine followed by a low tumbling. Then he begins to drive, slowly at first, pulling out onto the almost empty street. Sundown is here, it's the sabbath in Jerusalem, and the streets are empty. When we drive away, I see a menorah in a window, candles blazing.

The bus is silent as we drive away.

CHAPTER SEVENTEEN

Rachel Grace (Dylan)

I T'S WELL PAST nightfall when the bus makes its way into Tel Aviv. You can see the city from a long way off, of course—unlike Jerusalem, which is fairly dark in the evening, the light pollution from the towers and high rises here is intense. The bus fights traffic, and those of us who stayed awake in the bus talk quietly, partly because several people went to sleep, and partly just... because. There's something a little sobering and sad about this ride.

The bus is just getting off the highway and onto the streets of Tel Aviv when Alex, who has been reading her email on her iPhone, suddenly gasps. Her eyes are wide when she looks up at me.

"Dylan..." she says, shaking.

"What? What is it?"

She hands me the phone.

It takes me a second to orient myself to her phone— I've never actually looked at email on her phone (or on any phone for that matter). Then it takes a second more before it settles in that the Julia the email is from is her sister Julia Wilson,

But it's the subject of the email that stuns me.

To: Alexandra <AlexLovesStrawberries@yahoo.com>
From: Julia <Julia@morbidenterprises.com>
Subject: Progress
Dear Alex,

Our detective, Bill Nancy, called me this evening with progress. Over the last few days he's been visiting homeless shelters and camps in the Atlanta area. He had the picture you sent me of Dylan, and when he finally met some people who knew Dylan, he started asking about his friend. Social security, police and newspaper records turned up nothing about anyone named Spot, of course, but yesterday we got a hit.

A girl named Rachel Grace Bell from Norcross, Georgia was arrested by the Atlanta police last year and charged with misdemeanor possession of marijuana. Bill spoke with the arresting officer. Rachel Bell went by the street name Spot. She spent one month at the Metro Regional Youth Detention Center in Atlanta. The officer remembered her well.

Unfortunately, he's not sure what happened to her after that. But now that he has her name and other information, there's a better chance of finding out what happened.

I've attached a picture. Ask Dylan to verify if this is the girl he's looking for.

Love you,
Julia

As I read the email my heart is racing. I can't quite figure out my reaction, because I've got this crazy stupid mix of anticipation, of fear, even of anger at Alex. I'm confused how her sister Julia became involved.

I tell myself to not be an asshole. She was trying to help.

The attachment to the email is a mug shot. It's Spot. Or rather, it's *Rachel*. Crazy, that in the time I knew her, she never said her name. In the picture, she doesn't look good at all. She had a nasty shiner, and her hair had that flat, dull look people get when they haven't been eating or sleeping well enough. I take a deep breath.

Alex grabs my arm. "Are you okay?"

I nod. "Yeah. Yeah I am. That's... that's her. Can you send me that email?"

She nods. "Of course."

I almost don't want to know what happened to her. I'm afraid I'll find out it was something horrible. I shake my head. "She was a good friend," I say.

"I know," Alex whispers.

I failed her. Why didn't I just bring her home with me when I went back to school? Mom would have taken her in. I'm sure of it.

Rachel Grace Bell. What happened to you? I stare out of the bus into the darkness, trying to imagine what might have happened to her. Maybe that asshole who was beating her up at the Masquerade that night finally caught up with her and killed her. Or one of the predators. Every once in a while you'd see them, cruising around in the bad neighborhoods and homeless camps. Looking for girls like Rachel, because they could be forced into prostitution.

I'd break someone's fucking neck.

I swallow. The pain of failing her hurts my chest. I was never able to protect anyone—not my mother, when that bastard used to beat her up, not Spot. It kills me. I wish I could just be ... better somehow.

"What's wrong?" Alex asks. Her voice is filled with concern, compassion.

"Nothing," I say. "I'm fine."

But inside, I'm not. I'm not fine at all.

You're Crying (Alex)

The next morning is grey and cold. It's Saturday, December 7, and tomorrow morning we get on a plane to fly back to the United States.

Tomorrow I have to say goodbye.

I feel a sense of almost terror as I get ready for the brunch this morning. I'm sharing a room in the hostel with Elle, and she's fussing about something, but all I can think about is saying goodbye to Dylan.

I can't say goodbye. I don't want to say goodbye. I don't want to lose him.

I shake my head and drop onto the lower bunk in the room, not really listening as Elle prattles on about God only knows what. I'm shaking.

I don't really notice when Elle stops talking. But next thing I know, she's kneeling in front of me and her hands are gripping mine. "Alex, what's wrong?"

I shake my head, unable to control the tears that are running down my face. "Nothing," I say.

She twists her face in a look of extreme skepticism. "Nothing? Your eyes are just running water like that for … what?"

I sniff, making a gross sound that would have had my mother screaming, *Go blow your nose!* Serves her right, having six daughters. I say, "I don't... I can't... I ... I..."

That was really articulate, Alex. I try to talk, but I can't, because the tears are now running completely out of control.

"Oh, honey," Elle says. She leans forward and puts her arms around me, a sisterly sort of motion which I'm sure is completely alien. Or maybe she's decided to join the human race somehow. Or...

"It's Dylan, isn't it?" she asks.

I nod my head urgently.

"What did he do?" she asks.

"What?" I cry.

"What did he do to you?" she asks.

"He didn't do anything! I just... I don't want to say goodbye."

"Oh..." she says, her mouth forming a perfectly shaped O. She says, "I didn't realize you guys were *that* serious."

That's because you never look at anything but mirrors, Elle.

Elle presses forward acting like a friend. "Listen, you just need to talk with him. He graduates high school in a few months, and you do a year later. Just ... go to college in the same place. It's not so hard to figure out, Alex."

It's so much more complicated than that, I want to say. How can I suggest we go to college in the same place when he's never even said he loves me?

For that matter, I've never said it either. Are we going to go home and pretend it never happened? Are we going to go home and just... give up?

No. That's not okay. It's not. But where do I start?

I finally get my tears under control. It isn't easy. But the thing is, we've got a full day ahead of us. And I am *not* spending my last day with Dylan crying all day. Not. Going. To. Happen.

By the time we leave for the dining hall, I've put myself back together. We make our way downstairs. The room has a dozen large round tables, all of them crowded with students—not just the Americans, but all three sets of our host students for the last six weeks. I spy several people I've befriended—mousy little Hadar, American-born Lilah, Rebekah from Jerusalem. They're all at the same table, which is awkward, because Lilah is directly across the table from Yossi, who sits next to Dylan.

Dylan saved a seat for me, and when he spots me, he comes to his feet. For just a second I feel like the whole world goes silent when he stands. I approach, anxiety tearing me up inside.

How can I say goodbye? The thought of it almost brings tears, but I hold them back. Instead, I walk forward, and take his hand. He leans close and kisses the side of my mouth.

"Hey, beautiful," he says, and everything is all right.

For the next two hours, we have a brunch. I get to catch up with my friends—Hadar is unchanged. Ariel apparently is on the outs with everyone because of what happened when we were in Ramat Gan, so that at least is good news. Not that I wish bad things for him (I don't) but that kind of thing doesn't stop unless people *make* it stop.

Meanwhile, we get to hear speeches. The deputy assistant something or other from the US Embassy, Michael Terry, spots me at the table and walks over. They don't pay these guys to forget faces—he fusses for a few minutes, wishes my parents his best and then goes up front to give his speech. As he drones on about some obscure policy stuff, Dylan leans over and says, "Family friend?"

I shake my head. "No idea who he is. He must know my Dad."

Dylan nods and squeezes my hand.

After Terry comes the deputy mayor of Ramat Gan, then some woman from the Israel-America Friendship League. They all talk forever. I'm serious. Forever. Dylan sneaks off *twice* during the speeches to go smoke. It almost makes *me* want to go light up. If the hostel hadn't run out of food, they'd probably still be speaking. But it's finally over, and Mrs. Simpson calls us all together.

It's our last day in Israel. She gives us the rest of the day free. There will be a goodbye party this evening—informal, no dignitaries, thank goodness. But in the meantime, we're free to go wherever we want as long as we stay in the city.

Elle and John immediately suggest heading back to the pier in Jaffa. Mike joins us, loping along slightly hunched over, chatting with the much shorter Megan, who somehow found the time to die her hair a brilliant blue this week.

Dylan and I both take deep breaths at that suggestion. And of course it makes sense. That was our first night in the country, our first time really connecting.

"Yes," I say. "Let's go."

Dylan doesn't actually say anything, just nods. I don't go change into a bathing suit. We've been swimming a couple of times this trip, but today it's too cold. I'll go to the beach wearing a good sweater and jacket.

It's slow going getting there. Elle and I stop and shop in two different stores. I buy Dylan a silly tourist t-shirt, and we stop half a dozen times to get our pictures taken in front of buildings, in front of traffic, just — anywhere. Because we both know we don't want to go.

Dylan is quiet. But John and Elle make up for it, both of them talking a mile a minute. They're both from New York, and a few minutes ago they were discussing introducing each other to their friends, to their families. They must have gotten back together when I wasn't looking.

I won't even pretend I'm not jealous that they get to stay together.

We finally reach the beach. Dylan positions himself with his back to a low stone wall. I lean back against him, my back to his chest, his arms around me. John chases Elle down the beach. Mike and Megan—not a couple—look awkwardly at each other, then shrug and wander down the beach together.

Dylan and I don't talk. We just sit, his arms around me. I listen to the surf, the waves coming up the beach, whitecaps crashing against the pier. A tear slides down my face again. I can't stop it. I try. But I just can't.

I lean back, burying my face against his neck.

He says in a low voice. "You're crying."

I sniff and say, "You're full of astute observations."

Without hesitation he shifts his fingers into evil little claws and tickles my sides. I shriek, and then we're laughing, and then he's looking in my eyes, and he leans forward and his lips touch mine, and now we're kissing, his lips hard against mine.

I want to say it. I want to say the words. *I love you.* They catch in my throat, because he's never said it either, and if I say it and he doesn't then where does *that* leave me? I don't know if he even wants to try to stay together when we go home. What if he doesn't? Long distance relationships suck. They fall apart. They never last.

Dylan's kisses move, his lips slipping to my neck, and I lean my head back and close my eyes.

We stay that way for a long time, sometimes just sitting together, sometimes kissing. After a while, Megan and Mike return, and the four of us chat, then Elle and John show up. Me and Dylan wade out into the Mediterranean—which is *cold*—me trying to hold my skirt above the water, his pants rolled up to his knees. Megan takes a picture of us on my phone. Later, when a flock of seagulls lands on the pier, Dylan runs out there, arms waving, and the birds take off in a great rustling cloud, calling out their alarm to each other.

It's around four in the afternoon when we finally begin to make our way back to the hostel. We're all quiet, and we move slowly, stopping every few minutes to look at things, some unique, some common, but all of which we'll never see again together. The wind whips down Dizengoff Street, blowing dust right into our faces as we move toward the hostel again. Elle and John keep talking in low tones, but I feel impossibly awkward because Dylan is so quiet. I *need* to know what is happening with him. I need to know what he's thinking about, but he isn't talking and it's driving me insane.

All the same, I keep tight hold of his hand.

What do you want to do? (Dylan)

When we get back to the hostel, we agree to meet back downstairs in an hour. I only reluctantly let go of Alex, but there is a party coming, and she's gotta go do whatever it is girls do before parties. I, on the other hand, am going to grab a nap.

I go up to the room and just lay down on my side and stare at the wall. John says something—I don't know what—but I ignore him. He primps and puts gel in his hair and puts on so much cologne it makes my eyes burn. I don't know if I should do all that. What are you supposed to do when you're in love with a girl and have to say goodbye?

You tell her, asshole.

Yeah. That's a plan. Break both of our hearts. Sounds like fun.

I close my eyes and pretend to sleep. But I can't actually sleep. All I can do is see the last six weeks. Our flight over from New York. Our first night in Jaffa. Alex storming away after I intervened with Ariel, and Alex saying *I do* when I told her I liked her (*loved*) and asked her if she felt the same way. I see all those moments together—kissing at En Gedi, walking along the top of Masada, looking in her eyes, holding her in my arms.

Maybe, when I graduate, I should go to California. I could get a job out there, maybe take a couple of classes. I want to travel and write. San Francisco *is* travel. I've never been there, and it's supposed to be an amazing city.

Of course, she wants to go to college in New York or Boston. And wouldn't it be a little weird for me to follow her around from state to state? *That* doesn't make a whole lot of sense either.

How do I tell her how much I love her?

This is agonizing.

Finally, in frustration, I get up. I grab a quick shower in an effort to make myself presentable, then go upstairs to the rooftop. There's a small garden area up here, with lounge chairs and a picnic table, and two vaguely twenty-ish girls are leaning on each other on one of the benches.

It's full dark now, and I can hear the traffic in the street below, horns honking. It sounds as busy as New York did. It makes me miss the relative quiet of Jerusalem. I light a cigarette and sit down in one of the plastic chairs.

Rachel Grace Bell. I'm trying to comb through my emotions about learning Spot's real name. I don't exaggerate when I say that she was, in some ways, like a little sister to me. So senseless that she would die so young. She's younger even than Alex.

Was. She *was* younger than Alex.

I check my watch. It's six-thirty. Time to head down for the party and dinner. I move slowly and thoughtfully, with all the deliberation of an arthritic old man. Or someone headed for the gallows. I've got a strong sense of anxiety as I head downstairs—I've never been one for parties in the first place, and this one is likely to be not the most cheerful of experiences. I imagine at least some of our former host students will be at the party—most likely the ones from Ramat Gan, if no one else. But a much bigger deal than that is all the impending drama.

Not that I don't have enough drama of my own.

The main hall of the hostel is crowded when I enter. Students from all the groups are here, along with friends, host students and all the chaperones. Mrs. Simpson is somewhere near the front of the room, busily talking with a chaperone from one of the other groups. I look around, but I don't see Alex at first.

At first. But when I spot her, I stop cold.

She's wearing a form-fitting ankle length dress. It's a deep green that makes her eyes look almost luminous. She rarely wears makeup, but she has some on tonight. I have trouble breathing as I approach her.

"You look amazing," I say.

She smiles as I take her hands.

We're buffeted by all the people. John and Elle pop up. He's obviously drunk, and she's well on her way. John puts a hand on my shoulder and says, way too loud, "Buddy, it's your last chance to get her panties off!"

Elle slugs him and I almost do the same. But the two of them slip away, leaving me and Alex in the most awkward silence.

Ever.

Megan comes over, along with another girl I barely know, and they're chatting with Alex, and I find myself fading into the background a little. They keep talking, so I excuse myself to go grab a cigarette. This time I don't go to the roof, instead I just step out front of the building. I light a cigarette, and pace back and forth. It's dark, and there's a lot of traffic. People walk by on their way to coffee shops and restaurants, wholly unaware that right here my whole life is coming to a crashing end.

I go back in and we make the rounds. Alex and I find ourselves in a group with Rebekah, Alex's host student from Jerusalem, and Yossi, mine from Haifa. They're making eyes at each other, and as our conversation proceeds longer and longer, they sit closer and closer to each other. Alex nudges me at one point when Yossi goes to get them both drinks. I nudge her right back.

Soon after, I'm standing outside yet again, smoking a cigarette. Pacing. Trying to figure out what to say to Alex. Because the thing is, when we started this whole business out, we knew it was temporary. It was only for a few weeks. We weren't going to be something permanent, because that's impossible. But as the weeks have gone on, I've realized that in Alex I have something I could never have imagined. I have someone who I can see spending not just today or this week or this month with. No—she's someone I can imagine spending my *life* with.

In the back of my head, the peanut gallery shouts stupid objections. She's just turned seventeen, I'm eighteen. Neither of us knows what we want out of life. She's planning to go to college at an Ivy League in the heart of Manhattan—I'm planning on traveling and writing and maybe getting around to college whenever. We come from shockingly different backgrounds. Her father's a freaking ambassador, while mine probably has a felony conviction if he's even alive.

That stops me cold. I don't think about my dad often, because really he's not worth thinking about.

But I've seen the pictures. Mom doesn't know it. But back when I was still smoking pot I snuck in her room one time looking for cash. In the back of one of her drawers I found not cash, but a wedding photo album.

Larry Paris was a handsome man when he was young. My parents didn't have a fancy wedding—after all, they were way too young to be having kids, way too young. My Mom would have graduated high school in 1988, but she had me instead. Dad was a couple years older, and like me, he was a high school dropout. Like his son after him, he was a drunk.

The thing is, in those pictures in the photo album, they were only a year or so older than me and Alex. Only a year or so older, and so obviously in love.

They were in love. Deeply, passionately. And seven years later, he was punching her in the face because she talked back.

I can't do this. I can't fucking do this. I turn around, ready to storm back into the hostel, but instead I come face to face with Alex.

My resolve to walk away from her instantly crumbles.

"Alex," I say.

She looks up at me, concern writ on her face. "What's wrong, Dylan?"

I take a breath and just stare, struggling for an answer. She grabs my arms and says, "Come sit. Please. We need to talk."

I follow her. Two benches face each other, too close really, near the front entrance of the hostel. We sit facing each other. I swallow, then light a cigarette, because that's easier than talking.

Her eyes blink, and she looks — confused, her eyebrows drawn down close. "Dylan, talk to me. What's wrong?"

I look up at the sky. I don't know how to answer. Too many words are jumbled in my head. I open my mouth and stop. Then I do it again. *Christ.*

"Dylan..."

I finally get a word out. "Alex—the thing is... I know we said we were only temporary..."

She suddenly looks deeply apprehensive. I stop talking.

"What is it, Dylan?"

I take a deep drag off my cigarette, then say, "Alex... I don't know what to do from here. Are we just going to go home and pretend none of this ever happened? Are we going to go back to dating people we don't even like? Or... do we stay together? I don't see how that can work!"

She leans closer to me. Her eyes are watering, just a little.

I stand up and pace for a second. "Alex... I don't know what to do!" I stamp my cigarette out, then turn back toward her and sit down on the bench.

Her question cuts right through my apprehension. "What do you *want* to do?"

I struggle for an answer. Because what I *want* to do is kiss her and never ever let go. But I can't get my words around it. I can't spit it out. She moves suddenly to the bench I'm on, facing me, and *hits me* right in the chest with her fists.

"Why can't you tell me how you feel?" she shouts.

I blurt out my response suddenly. "Because I love you!"

Chapter Eighteen

Because I love you (Alex)

BECAUSE I LOVE you!

He really said that. I didn't mean to hit him, I just got so frustrated, and then he blurted *that* out. I feel my chin start to quiver uncontrollably, and then tears are running down my face and *I hate that I cry so damn much* and I say, "I love you too."

"You do?" he asks, looking shocked.

"Yes, idiot. I love you. I *love you.*"

Then we're kissing, and I'm still crying, and we're kissing more. Our lips come apart for a moment—just long enough for him to say, "Alex, I love you," and then we're kissing again, our lips pressed together. One of his hands is at the small of my back, pulling me to him.

I don't know how long the kiss lasted. I know it was a long, long time. Cars passed by, an eternity passed by. I felt a fat raindrop hit my face, then another. I ignored them, concentrating only on him.

He broke away from me, just by a few centimeters. I say, "You still haven't answered my question. What do *you* want to do?"

His voice is ragged when he responds. "I want us to try. I … I know it's long distance, we live thousands of miles apart. I know we've got sort of different plans for after high school, and I know your dad will probably hire secret agents to have me killed, but... I want us to try it. I don't care if the odds are against us. You're worth it."

I nod, feeling tears threatening again. "We're worth it," I say.

"It's not going to be easy," he says.

"Why should everything be easy?" I reply.

"We'll stay in touch online. And call each other. And I'll come visit."

Then we're kissing again. It's an urgent kiss, our bodies pressed against each other in an effort to fill the void we both know is coming. More rain splatters against me, one drop, then another, then another. The wind, already high this afternoon, is picking up even more.

In a haze, we get up and move back into the hostel.

Forgotten ghost (Dylan)

My watch starts to beep its alarm at 5 am. I quickly reach over and silence it.

Alex is asleep. We stayed up talking until 1, then came up here. John wasn't back—and we both had the feeling he wasn't coming back—so Alex stayed here with me. We talked more—Alex laying on her back, hands clasped across her stomach. That posture, of course, pushed her breasts against her sweater in a way that made me very intensely aware of her every move. We talked and she laughed and I laughed—and she cried a little. We kissed so much that my lips are chapped. I wanted to do more, but I didn't push—she's not ready for that yet.

Asleep, she looks so pure. Her long eyelashes arch gracefully, her lips turned up in the faintest of smiles. About an hour ago she turned over to face me, bringing her knees up in front of her, her hands together almost in an attitude of prayer in front of her face. In a slow rhythm, not unlike the sea a few blocks away, her breath rises and falls.

I've been watching her. I couldn't sleep. I keep telling myself that we'll make it, that this isn't it, that when we say goodbye it won't be the end, it will just be a brief intermission before we're together again. In my heart, I'm terrified. I don't even want to take my eyes off of her, not even for a second, because I'm terrified life is going to snatch her right out of my arms. I lay facing her, my left hand on her waist.

I love you.

That's the words that run through my mind every time I look at her face. I can hear her saying it, over and over again as we kissed.

I love you.

She stirs a little—the alarm disturbed her. She opens her eyes for just a second. I whisper, "You've got a little while to sleep."

She whispers back, "I love you, Dylan." Her eyes are already closed again, fast asleep.

It seems hardly fair, that I get to have her. After all, who am I? I'm just some guy. Nothing unusual about me except that my dad abused my mom and then she kicked him out, and let's face it, there's nothing special about that.

Alex—she's just about the most beautiful girl I've ever seen in my life. Every time I look at her long silky brown hair, her flawless skin, emerald eyes, I can only think that somehow I got mixed up in someone else's fate. Like I've inherited the life of someone who I'm not—someone strong, a hero, a knight who would some-day swoop in to protect her.

I'm not those things, but I'll do my best to live up to them. I'll do my best to deserve her.

It's 5:30 now, and her breath is slow and deep. I can just barely make out her eyes moving under the eyelids. She's dreaming.

I try to picture what her dreams must be like. I wonder if I'm in them? She stays that way for what feels like a long time. Her body jerks a couple of times, just a tiny bit, as if she's startled. But then she subsides, her breath shortening, and her eyes open slightly.

For a few seconds I'm caught up in the wonder of her eyes. Then I say, "Good morning, beautiful."

She smiles. "I dreamt about you."

"How did you sleep?" I ask.

"I've never slept better." She looks shy as says the words.

"I love you," I say.

"I thought you were never going to say it." She sits up just a little, resting on her elbows. "It's getting lighter. Is it time?"

"It's getting close. A little after 5:30."

"I need to go pack my bags," she says.

I'm irrationally unhappy that she has to go, even if it's just for a few minutes. I don't want to let her out of my sight.

She leans close to me, and whispers, "I want you to know, this was the best night of my life, Dylan."

"Mine too." With that, she slips out of the room.

Twenty minutes later we meet in the dining hall downstairs. Everyone is quiet, all too aware that this is the last meal we will share as a group. That this is the last morning we'll spend together. Across the table from me, Elle leans against John, her face streaked with tears.

I study them for a second. John looks as sober as I've ever seen him. He eats with his left hand, keeping his right hand wrapped around her waist. My heart is heavy. It's hard for me to imagine what it's going to be like going home. I have friends back in Atlanta, people I care about, but they seem so distant in the last weeks. I've never had anyone like Alex.

After breakfast, we gather our bags and move to the bus out front, like prisoners shambling to their execution. For the last time we load our bags on the bus, get on board, and find our seats. As she often does, Alex leans on me and closes her eyes.

It's not raining outside anymore, but it feels like it could start again any minute. The wind whips up the street, shaking trees and branches, and blowing a plastic bag end over end down the street, like a forgotten ghost.

Alex snuggles closer, and I wrap my arms around her.

It's her (Alex)

I slept most of the flight to New York.

We barely slept at all last night, and to be honest, I think it was easier that way. During the bus ride to Ben-Gurion airport outside Tel Aviv, I could feel my heart breaking. And so, most of the flight, the armrest between our seats was lifted, and I slept leaning on Dylan's lap. I don't think he slept at all. Because every time I woke up, he was sitting there looking at me, an expression of love in his eyes.

Our flight had a layover in London. It was two hours. Not enough time to explore or do anything. Dylan and I, with Elle and John, sat around a table having a cup of coffee and playing cards. No one really wanted to talk, because we were all feeling the same way, but didn't want to acknowledge it.

Then we got back on the plane, and here we are. When the plane touches the ground with a bounce and slight screech of tires, the passengers erupt in applause. I've heard it before—it's surprisingly common when an international flight touches down in the United States. I have an ache in my chest, and my stomach turns. I lean against Dylan. The plane is taxiing to the gate. We're back in the United States.

"What time is your flight to Atlanta?"

"In an hour. What about you? When do you have to be at your sister's?"

"She's expecting me soon. I'm going to call and tell her I'm not coming until after your flight leaves. "

The thought of his flight leaving makes my stomach turn. The engines on the plane begin to wind down, and I hear a thump as the moving walkway connects to the plane.

We are in the back of the plane, so it's going to be a little while. I stay close to Dylan. Ellie comes back to our seats, and asks, "How long are you going to stay in New York, Alex?"

"Just three days. I'll be staying at my sister's apartment near Columbia."

Ellie says, "I'll call you. Let's have lunch before you go?"

We follow the line of passengers off the plane. Most of our connecting flights are leaving out of the same area of the airport, except for the group from Milwaukee. They are going to have to run, in order to make their flight on time. Dylan won't have long either—it takes us nearly twenty minutes to get off the plane.

Megan throws her arms around me, crying, tears pouring down her face.

"I'll miss you," she says.

"I'll miss you too," I croak, my voice breaking up.

Megan hugs Dylan and John and Ellie as the chaperone for Milwaukee calls, "Come on, we're going to be late!"

And then they are gone. Megan, the last of the group, runs as fast as she can down the corridor.

"I'm going to call my sister," I say. I take out my phone and switch it on. It takes a minute to start. then it pops up an alert. Two new voicemails.

One of the calls is from Carrie. I don't recognize the other phone number, from the 404 area code. I don't know where that is. I start to press the button to listen to the message but my phone starts ringing.

It's from the same 404 area code number. I answer.

"Hello? "

"Hello… I'm trying to reach Alex Thompson, " The voice is female, young, and has a southern accent considerably thicker than Dylan's.

"This is she," I reply.

"My name is Rachel. I was told that you're with Dylan, and that he is looking for me."

I gasp. *It's her!* "He's right here," I say, my voice shaking a little. I lower my hand with the phone, and I say to Dylan, "This call is for you."

His eyebrows draw together in a quizzical expression. But he takes the phone, puts it to his ear, and says, "this is Dylan."

He listens for one second, then staggers, eyes suddenly shining with tears.

I Promise (Dylan)

When I hear the words, "Dylan, this is Spot," I feel as if someone punched me in the gut. A rush of emotions floods through me. Confusion, love, and incredible relief. I sink into one of the plastic chairs bolted into the floor, my eyes on Alex in wonder as I reply.

"Spot? It's really you?"

"I don't actually go by that anymore," she says. "That was part of the different life."

"Rachel, then? That's what Alex's sister said your name is."

"That's right," she says. "Rachel."

"Scott—told me that you were dead."

"I'm not surprised he thought so. I did my best to leave all of that behind."

"What happened?"

"Nothing all that special. I got arrested. When I got out, I went to my parents. I didn't know where else to go, and Dylan... I was afraid to be out on the streets again, and I didn't know where you were."

I asked her, "What did they say? Are they still treating you wrong? You can come stay—"

"Dylan, it's okay. It really is."

Relief. I ask, "What did they say?"

She sniffs, loudly. "Dad ... when he saw me ... he fell on his knees. And he begged me to forgive him."

Oh my God. "Sp—Rachel, I'm so happy. I'm *so* happy. I thought you were dead."

"No. I'm back home now. I... I'd like to see you when you get home, if that's okay. But only if you're not doing that stuff anymore... I quit getting high."

"Me too."

We exchange phone numbers, and I promise to call her, and we hang up. I find myself rubbing my eye with the palm of my hand. Alex touches me on the shoulder. "Your friend is alive," she says. Her smile is amazing.

I force back the watering in my eyes. "Thank you, Alex. *Thank you.*" I can't say how much it means. That on some level I blamed myself for her not getting help, not finding her way home. I blamed myself for not going back that first day after I moved home, so I could help her too.

She puts her hands on both sides of my face and says, "You know I'd do anything for you."

I meet her eyes. "And I would for you."

She swallows and whispers, "I don't want to say goodbye."

I close my eyes for a second to force back the emotion spilling over. "I don't either. I don't ever want to say goodbye to you."

I hear the call over the loudspeakers. "Flight 704 to Atlanta, boarding at gate B39."

"That's your flight," she croaks out, her voice cracking. Tears pour down her face as she says the words. Jesus Christ.

"I can skip it," I say. "I don't have anything to do in Atlanta anyway."

She snorts, but doesn't stop crying. "Except graduate high school?"

"Yeah," I say. "There's that."

We lean together, foreheads touching, tears mingling. "This isn't it," I say. "Not by a long shot. I don't know whether it's next month or next year or … or what… but we will be together."

"Promise me," she says.

Boarding rows 29 to 40, Flight 704 to Atlanta. Please have your tickets out and ready. The words punch into me, far weightier than they have any right to be.

"I promise," I say. "I promise I'm your forever. I promise I'll come find you wherever you are. I promise."

"Please don't forget me," she whispers.

"I could never forget you."

We kiss, eyes closed, the whole world blocked out. I've never felt so—so torn, my heart lacerated. Every bit of my being is with *her* and I don't want to go. *I don't want to go.*

"Dylan, it's time to board the plane." I hear Mrs. Simpson's voice from a great distance.

Last call, Flight 704 to Atlanta, boarding now.

"Go!" Alex urges. "Go."

We break away from each other and I look deep in her eyes, trying to see, will she remember? Will she stay strong? Will I? I've got so many doubts and fears, so many questions. I look up to the gate. Mrs. Simpson is there now, waving urgently for me to come. A flight attendant is walking in my direction.

Shit. Time to go.

I turn back to Alex, meeting her eyes one last time, and I bring my fingers to her face with a feather touch.

Then I leave her, with two last words.

I promise.

Nickel Mines

(Crank and Julia Wilson, 2006)

A one room schoolhouse
Fields of grain
Soft sounds of rural life
Creaking of leather straps and wagon wheels
Manure and hickory smoke

The wind blows metallic terror
as a truck backs up into a nightmare
A man
torn by
                something?

"I'm trying to find something he says"
to disarm
then he brings out the guns
The clatter of rounds in the chamber
A threat revealed

Some escape
Some are let go
adults with babies, and all the boys
hot with fear and sweat

but the girls are kept in quivering terror
zip ties cut into the flesh
trembling faith stretched thin by evil

Some real or imagined offense
far in the man's past
brings murder to Nickel Mines

take me first, says one girl, that the others may live
a second girl asks for the same

One shot, two, three, then four. Five and six. Seven.

Eight. Nine.

Ten.

Naomi and Lena. Mary Liz and Anna Mae. Marion
all dead

I would ask
did the killer believe in Jesus and
if so, was he whisked straight to heaven?

How do you get justice when someone kills themselves after mur-
dering children?

When it was all over
the families sought out the wife and children of the killer

                              and touched them
                              offered help
                              reconciliation
                              love

for the families, how is it that the first thing they did
was

                    forgive?

Going Home

(Dylan Paris, December 2007)

My thoughts are sharp, battering
through the mind.

Over the roar of engines I see sky,
grey as tensile steel. A shiver.

Breath is like a phantom,
waving in its white loneliness,
going nowhere.

The roar becomes a scream,
a scream in my heart,
magic turned cold.
Tears.

Over the pitching roar,
my life is torn apart,
the heart cries injustice.
As the rain begins.

Shambling on the plane,
sleep is welcome,
covering the bleeding void,
cool sweet darkness sweeps over,
anesthetic and warm.